BY ELSWYTH THANE

Fiction

RIDERS OF THE WIND
ECHO ANSWERS
CLOTH OF GOLD
HIS ELIZABETH
BOUND TO HAPPEN
QUEEN'S FOLLY
TRYST
REMEMBER TODAY
FROM THIS DAY FORWARD
MELODY
THE LOST GENERAL

The Williamsburg Novels

DAWN'S EARLY LIGHT
YANKEE STRANGER
EVER AFTER
THE LIGHT HEART
KISSING KIN
HOMING (*in preparation*)

Non-Fiction

THE TUDOR WENCH
YOUNG MR. DISRAELI
ENGLAND WAS AN ISLAND ONCE
THE BIRD WHO MADE GOOD
RELUCTANT FARMER

Plays

THE TUDOR WENCH
YOUNG MR. DISRAELI

The Lost General

The
Lost General

by
ELSWYTH THANE

BEEBE

AEONIAN PRESS, INC.
NEW YORK, 1974

C. 1 c

For
Monica McCall

Acknowledgments

As usual, I encountered technical difficulties in the construction of the book, and had to take legal and medical advice. I am grateful to Mr. André Maximov and Dr. Harold Foster for the time spent in answering the questions of a layman in their respective fields. The seed of this story has been cherished ever since my first trip to South Carolina some years ago during the research on *Dawn's Early Light,* but setting a modern book in a part of the country where I was not myself a native presented problems. Miss Marguerite Steedman has taken endless trouble to preserve me from committing solecisms in the Southern scene.

E. T.

The Lost General

I

HE HAD PERISHED OBSCURELY IN ONE OF those footling little skirmishes outside Charleston in 1782, when the war for American Independence was theoretically over. Cornwallis had surrendered at Yorktown the year before, but the British garrisons still held on in Charleston, Savannah, and New York. Neither Greene in his South Carolina headquarters nor Washington at Newburgh had enough wherewithal to attack them and throw them out.

He was a young general, and full of fight, and he ventured once too often on a chancy forage raid and was carried into a white wooden church near a ford to die. Some ammunition was stored in the church, and some hay for the officers' horses, and between the two, and nothing to do with the dead general, the church caught fire and burned to the ground.

The history books said that there was now no trace of the church, nor of the few tombstones which might have been near it, nor was it known where the General's body had finally been laid to rest. But Mary Carmichael, twenty-two, knew that history books could be wrong, and she had come all the way from Massachusetts to look for the General's grave. It was a sentimental journey, purely. She could have written her thesis on the General's life without it, if she had not fallen in love with him.

He had been dead a hundred and seventy years when she set out alone in her little car in search of him, and everybody said she was crazy. But that didn't stop her, because Mary was a stubborn girl, and she had enough money of her own to provide a holiday each year if she didn't spend it all on clothes and fripperies, which there was little temptation to do as she hadn't anything that could rightly be called a beau.

Mary had been brought up by her widowed mother and her spinster aunt, who naturally chose to send her to an exclusively female college to learn to be a professor in some other female college. To complete the handicap, the college she attended was in the same town, so that she naturally lived off campus, at home. And there she was always given to understand that men, as such, were negligible socially and a nuisance around the house.

So far, she didn't appear to question the verdict, though she did hear something to the contrary now and then. Some of the other girls had brothers, of course, at boys' colleges, and they sometimes went through the obliging motions of "finding a man" for Mary. But she was shy, and her dates seldom took, like her vaccinations. She was not at ease at dances, stage-fright made her pretty useless at sports, and while she was attractive in a mousy way, men — that is

[4]

to say, boys — were inclined to overlook her. They had no way of knowing that she could cook like an angel, and liked to. So Mary at twenty-two really knew very little about men, even as uncles — there weren't any uncles in her family.

But Mary had the General.

She had picked him out of the back pages of a history of the American Revolution, and from there had tracked him devotedly through other men's memoirs and other men's *Lives* — he was mentioned often, and with praise, but his own biographies were confined to footnotes and a column in the D.A.B. And always there was that touching bit about the place of his burial being unknown.

Her determination to go and look for it as part of the source material for her thesis was viewed with endless alarm by her mother and her aunt, who offered to go with her, singly or *en masse*, and warned her that the South was not safe for a woman travelling alone. At the price of hurt feelings and disapproving silences and a resentment which followed her for miles, she had extricated herself from their chaperonage and cautionary tales, and driven away on a warm April day with a simple wardrobe in one suitcase, a kit which held two picnic bottles and a tin box for sandwiches, her money in travellers' checks and the car running like silk. It was the Easter vacation, and she had nearly two weeks.

She took Mount Vernon on the way, though it had nothing to do with her General, and Williamsburg, though he had never seen it, and crossed by the ferry at Jamestown, singing with excitement and freedom, for she had never been so far afield before without back-seat driving. There had been no Advances, though garage attendants and hotel clerks had not beheld her with complete indifference. She wasn't tall and she had a heart-shaped kitten face with a short nose and a generous mouth. Her light brown hair was young and soft and shining, cut with a casual wave, and she seldom wore a hat. But she knew where she was going, her manner was a trifle formal, and it was hard to catch her eye. They left her alone.

She drove straight down the coast to Wilmington in North Carolina and then began to putter, using the map and the back roads, southwards towards Charleston. It was not easy for her to make friends with strangers even when she wanted to, because she was shy, but she found that waitresses and hotel clerks and people in filling stations were willing to talk about their local landmarks, and a kind of folk-lore began to emerge, as one thing led to another.

At a small, clean, gracious hotel in a small South Carolina town she was directed to a house called Chimneys, which traditionally had sheltered her General the night before the fatal skirmish. It was owned by two elderly spinster sisters, she was told, who took paying guests for the wild duck and turkey season and the deer hunting — people from the North mostly, it was mentioned with tact, who probably had never heard of the General; they came for the shooting and the old-fashioned Southern hospitality which the Misses Sibley provided, with a discreet bill at the end of the stay —

a bill, it might have been mentioned, of fabulous size, but no one would have dreamed of complaining and everyone actually considered that they had had their money's worth in atmosphere and charm.

A telephone call was made by the hotel on Mary's behalf, and she drove out to the house called Chimneys, where she was cordially received by two picture-book old ladies who gave her tea and homemade cake and showed her the room the General might have slept in. Everything in the house seemed to be made of lustrous mahogany, and its brass and silver shone with loving care. No one would ever have guessed that it was all done by one ancient colored woman, an only slightly younger houseman and gardener, and Miss Theodosia and Miss Miranda, all working themselves to the knuckle in common bondage to the sacred traditions of Chimneys, and all more than contented to do so till they dropped.

Without much hope, Mary again brought up the matter of the church which had burned, and the burial place, and the two women glanced at each other with surprise and satisfaction.

"Now, fancy your knowing about that," said Miss Miranda. "The church is gone, of course — but you might find where it stood, the road still branches there. They do say — I think my father used to say — that the General's body was taken to a little burying ground a few miles away. But that's disappeared too, I expect, by now. Under the dam, no doubt, like a lot of other things."

"Dam?" Mary was at a loss.

They explained about the dam, which had gone in a few years before, flooding historic ground, ruining the value of inherited property, driving people out of homes they had occupied for generations. Their resentment of the dam was intense and personal. That they had escaped its ravages themselves was not the point. It had broken hearts, that dam. People had died of it.

Mary listened patiently about the dam.

"But the church," she reminded them finally. "Was its site flooded too?"

They thought not. In any case, there wasn't any church, hadn't been for years. The site should have had a marker. It was more important than other places where some Society or other had taken the trouble to put up a tablet.

"Could you show me on a map where the road forks?" she asked.

They were willing to try, but the motor map confused them. They fumbled and guessed and contradicted each other. In the end she encircled two possible spots with a pencil mark and drove back to the little hotel in town, where she had a bath and dinner and made up her notes.

It's getting nearer, she said almost aloud as she slid into bed. Tomorrow — next day — something will happen. Where the church was, maybe. Something will *come* to me. . . .

The next morning she set out again, with the picnic bottles full of hot tea, cheese and crackers and cookies in

[8]

the sandwich box, and a bag of fruit from the store. She always took her midday meal by the roadside, for it saved time and money, and sightseeing was hungry work. She found a place where the church ought to have been, but nothing came to her there, and no trace of foundations or tombstones remained in the undergrowth, which was full of poison ivy.

It was very hot for April, even in Carolina, and she ate her lunch under a tree further along the road and drove on, a little discouraged, in search of the other place they had put a pencil mark. Once more she drew blank, and it was mid-afternoon when she got into the car again and took the less travelled of two roads leading off into grateful shade under tall, moss-hung trees. Her expectation of some mysterious guidance had faded. But she followed the winding, little-used road idly, disappointed, feeling as though she had somehow lost the scent, wondering where to start again.

There was a house on the left side of the road. She slowed the car to look at it, impressed and saddened by its shabby grandeur. It was the kind of house you read about in books about the Old South — white columns, carriage sweep, live oaks festooned with moss, tall windows, exotic Southern flowers, and all. But it hadn't been painted for years, and its front garden was a wilderness with some perennial bloom struggling on. Except that there were curtains at the windows, and the wide front door stood open behind a screen door, it looked almost uninhabited.

It was no Chimneys, prosperous and burnished, but it might all the same contain some more old ladies, she thought, lingering in front of it. I could drive in, and see if anybody shows up, she thought. I wouldn't have to get out of the car if I didn't like the looks of them. It's just the kind of place where they would be likely to *know*. . . .

She drove between the weathered brick gate-posts and up to the broad steps.

She waited a minute, sitting in the car. There were no signs of life from within. It would be rude to blow the horn, as if it were a filling-station. Now that she was here, she might as well ask. . . .

She got out of the car and mounted the steps. There seemed to be no bell, so she knocked on the outer door-casing, faintly at first, then more boldly. Footsteps crossed a bare floor within, and a man in a white suit came through the shadowy hall towards the door. She spoke rather hurriedly through the screen.

"I'm sorry to bother you, but I thought someone here might help me. I'm looking for the church that burned, and the General's grave."

"We don't know where he's buried," a quiet voice answered without any surprise. "They lost him."

The man opened the door and stepped out on the porch instead of inviting her inside. He was taller than most men, and very slightly built, and his carriage failed to make the most of his height. His white suit was clean but limp and worn-looking, his face was fine-featured but colorless and unanimated, his blue eyes looked as though he had been asleep — maybe thirty, not much more — with that quiet, charming voice.

"I — heard something about a burying ground," she ventured, encouraged to go on with it by his tacit acceptance of her presence on such an errand.

"Where did you hear?" he asked indulgently, as though speaking to a precocious child.

"Two old ladies in the House where he stayed the night before he was killed."

"Oh, the Sibley girls," he said, enlightened, and a smile broke up the sombreness of his face, making him at once younger and wider awake. "Bless their hearts, they talk too much. Did they send you here?"

"Oh, no — I was looking for the church down where the road forks, and couldn't find a trace. So then I came on along this road, I don't quite know why, I just — You *do* know something about it!" she cried, searching his kind amusement with unself-conscious eagerness.

"I think I know the burying ground they mean. It just escaped the dam."

"I heard about the dam. Did it touch you here at all?"

"Most of the land we used to own is under it."

"Oh — I'm sorry." It seemed an inadequate thing to say. "But the burying ground escaped? Could I see it?"

"There isn't much to see. There's no marker for any general's grave, you know, although the legend that he is there does exist. And not all the graves are marked. The

General's could be one of those. A wooden marker which was not replaced would have disappeared now."

"Can I go there?"

"Not by car. It's back through the woods behind the house — fairly rough going."

"Could you — would you have time to show me the way?"

"I'd have the time, but — " His pleasant, impersonal glance went down to her nylon stockings and small but sensible shoes. "It's pretty rough," he warned her again.

"I wouldn't mind that — if you don't."

"Then come on." He moved forward and hesitated, seeming still a little doubtful. "That is — if you want to go now?"

"I would if it's convenient."

"Certainly." He left the door open and the screen unlatched, and started down the steps. "We can come into the path by going out through the yard at the back."

She walked beside him around the house and through a neglected rose garden not yet in bloom, across a sandy yard with a woodpile and an outside kitchen where there was a smell of pine burning in a stove. A rather casual-looking vegetable garden off at one side was being worked by a bent old colored man who paused to regard them with some surprise. There was a shabby car of inexpensive make in an open shed.

It occurred to her belatedly that they would not approve at home of her setting out alone with a perfectly strange man into perfectly strange woods. His innate courtesy, his rather listless and remote manner were reassuring, and yet — so listless was it, so dim and queer, that she entertained a passing thought that he might have been drinking instead of sleeping when she knocked at the door. But there was no odor of liquor, no outward sign that she could recognize. And it would be very foolish to pass up this opportunity out of childish caution. Surely he was what they called a gentleman. . . .

"How did you come to be looking up the General?" he inquired, holding open a dilapidated gate which separated the yard from the wilderness, so that she could pass him into a narrow grassy trail which wound away under the great moss-hung trees.

"I'm writing his life for my Master's thesis," she explained.

"I see," he said gravely. "That ought to be a valuable piece of work. There isn't an official *Life*, so far as I know."

"No, there isn't."

"It ought to be published."

"I don't suppose anybody would be interested. Unless I could find the grave. I thought — well, if I *discovered* something about him, I might get some interest — n-not for publishing my work, I don't mean that, it probably isn't worth much, but for putting up a monument and making it possible for people to find it — like Francis Marion's tomb, for instance — or even poor Marjoribanks up at Eutaw Springs."

"Poor Marjoribanks," he nodded with comprehension, and gave her a long glance full of interest.

"He died of wounds at the side of the road on the retreat, two days after the battle — so far from home — and they just buried him there. You can't but feel sorry for Marjoribanks, even though he wore a red coat."

"You know, if I may say so, you're a very unusual person to come out of Massachusetts."

So he had noticed the license plate. He wasn't, perhaps, as sleepy as he looked.

"I don't really consider myself a New Englander," she remarked. "I was born out West. When my father died my mother came back to her grandmother's home in Massachusetts because she and my aunt had inherited it jointly and we might as well live there. Have you lived here all your life?"

"Except for going away to school and then several years in the Pacific."

"Oh — the Pacific."

"Yes, but don't take it too hard, I didn't see much fighting. I was stuck away on one of those little forgotten islands, doing supply work. The poor man's South Pacific," he added wryly. "No enchanted evenings, no Bali H'ai. Just boredom and drudgery and discipline. When I got back here the dam had gone in and that was that. It's a lost world here now — what's left of it."

She wondered how he made a living, where he had gone to school, and whether he was married. She was silent so long, wondering, that he said anxiously, "Is this too much for you? It's only a little further."

"Oh, no — I'm not tired. I was thinking." She looked up to find him smiling at her over his shoulder. The path was now too narrow for them to walk side by side. "It's kind of you to take all this trouble for me," she said impulsively.

"On the contrary, I'm enjoying it. Tell me why you happened to settle on this particular general for your thesis."

"I was sorry for him. And then I got very fond of him."

"How nice of you," he said sincerely. "He has been a bit neglected."

"He grew on me. I read all his letters, and he came alive. They're in an appendix to a *Life* of somebody else, you know."

"I know. Got it on a shelf right there in the house," he said.

"Finally I felt as though I really *knew* him," she said, and stumbled, and he put out a quick, protecting hand which she ignored because she didn't need it. "I got so I could *think* for him — that is, it seemed as though I knew *how* he thought — he seemed to tell me things — I don't mean to sound silly and psychic, but that's how it was."

"You fell in love with him," he said gravely, as though it was not at all silly. "Wasn't there anyone else to fall in love with?"

"No. I guess that's why."

"What's the matter with them up in Massachusetts?" he asked, with another smiling glance.

[15]

"The boys? I don't know many."

"That's an odd state of affairs."

"Not if you live with your mother and your aunt, and always go to girls' schools, and haven't any male relatives. Men just don't occur to you, somehow. You don't miss them."

"Don't you? And what are you going to do with your life?"

"I'm going to teach, after I get my Master's this June."

"That seems rather a waste," he said. "The General would never have approved of that."

She laughed.

"No, I expect he was the kind of man who thought woman's place was in the home. Still, he never married."

"He hadn't time. But that doesn't say he was never in love."

"More than once, I should think! Women all adored him. There is that story about the Tory girl who warned him that Tarleton was coming and helped him to get away —"

"That happened just the other side of town, at a place called Bellington Bridge."

"How wonderful to find someone I don't have to explain everything to! Is that house still there?"

"Traces of it. The chimney, and part of the foundations. It caught fire about 1915, I think — people were still living in it at that time. Well, here you are, this is all there is."

He paused at the edge of a little enclosure in the wilderness. The gate in the rusted iron fence stood open. Great grey streamers of moss overhung it from the branches of trees so dense that the afternoon sunlight reached the ground only in confetti flecks of gold. The light was sub-dued yet luminous, as in a grotto, still, and dimly green. No breath of air stirred, and the heat was intense.

Grey stones, bronzed with lichen, were set at intervals, separated by irregular paths — sometimes a row of six or eight stones together, sometimes a pair of table tombs, an occasional shaft, chipped and discoloured. Some of the stones had fallen, or leaned askew.

The silence as they stood there was complete, unbroken by bird or insect.

"Isn't it beautiful," she murmured at last, and his eyes rested on her absorbed face with a kind of fascinated in-credulity and a growing tenderness. "M-may we go in?"

"Of course." He preceded her through the gateway and stood aside, watching her as she stepped slowly down a path between two lines of stones. Slowly he followed her, keep-ing a few steps between them, searching her face while she paused to read the inscriptions, watching her warily, as one watches a wild creature one fears to startle into flight.

"So many Crestons," she whispered, noting the recurrent name. "All come home to rest."

It was a long moment before he replied.

"That is my name," he said. "These are my people." He moved to stand at the end of a row where the rank grass and weeds had been kept from encroaching on more recent stones. "This is my father," he said simply, without any emotion. "He died just before I was born. My mother has never really recovered from the tragedy. This will be my place here," he said, looking down.

She was shocked and silent before his listless acquiescence in the brevity of human life. He strolled on, unhurried, oddly at home and at his ease, towards an unmarked grave, sunken rather than mounded, as very old graves are, which was placed a little apart from the rest.

"I like to think this may be the General," he said matter-of-factly. "It seems different somehow — outside the family groups."

She went to the edge of the enclosure and quickly gathered a handful of whatever small blooms she found there — except for a few violets they were straggling, commonplace, flowering weeds, but they were green and fresh and lovingly arranged — and returning, she knelt rather solemnly to lay them on the nameless grave.

"Just in case," she said, looking up at him from her knees beside it.

His hand rested lightly on her shoulder and was awkwardly withdrawn at once.

"I hope someone will do as much for me one day," he said.

His brief touch left her very still beside the grave, her head bent as if in prayer. Who was he, what was he, this unknown, disarming, courteous man with his lazy Southern vowels and soft voice, — a man in whom she felt no male strangeness, but only companionship and comprehension and — yes, a need like her own. It was as though she had known him always — known him the way she knew the General. And yet, as men there was no likeness between them. This man was not the kind she could ever admire, there was something lacking in him, something dimmed and helpless and lost — lost, like the General. . . .

She stood up, looking troubled and uncertain, and her eyes sought his, to find them waiting, not smiling now, but kind — so kind — and as though they asked something of her.

"You're very patient," she said gratefully. "We'll go now, I've taken up enough of your time."

"My time is not valuable," he said dryly. "Please believe me, I have enjoyed every minute of this."

They stood looking at each other between the grey stones in the eerie grotto light under the great trees. Each wanted to add something, and neither could speak.

"We must go back," she said, and stood still, looking at him.

"Yes, I suppose we must," he agreed, and with an effort he released her gaze from his and turned away towards the gate.

The return journey along the woods path was made almost in silence, and the sun was low when they came to the house again, and her car where she had left it below the steps.

"I have some books which might be of use to you, but unfortunately I can't ask you to come inside," he said formally

[19]

as they came out on to the overgrown drive. "My mother lives here with me, but she is away on a visit."

"I must get back to the hotel, I promised I wouldn't drive after dark." She held out her hand, retreating into the conventions native to them both, which prohibited her unchaperoned entrance into his house. "Good-bye. And thank you so much."

"It was a pleasure," he said. His fingers were quick and warm on hers.

She took a backward step towards the car and lingered again, glancing round as though to fix the scene in her memory.

"Has your house got a name?" she asked diffidently. "So many of them down here do have lovely names."

"Yes, it's called Fleetwood. After a place in England, as so many of them are."

"Oh, I like that — Fleetwood. And is that really a camellia, just growing on a bush?"

"Just about the last one this year." He reached out and broke off the small, belated red blossom from the bush near the porch, and as he stood looking down at it in his fingers she noticed that it trembled from the unsteadiness of the hand that held it.

"Of course you have seen the springs called the Fountain?" he suggested, without looking at her.

"Where the General's headquarters were? I wasn't sure they still existed. Are they near here?"

"Ten miles beyond, by this same road."

"Could we go there too?"

"Not today, if you want to see them properly and be back in town before dark."

"Tomorrow?"

"If you like."

They were looking at each other now, across the red camellia, with a feeling of mutual reprieve.

"In the morning?" she asked. "I'll bring along a picnic lunch. I always like to lunch beside the road."

"That would be — a good idea," he got out.

"What time shall I come? Ten? Eleven?"

"Whenever you like."

"Ten-thirty." She opened the door and slid into the car. "My flower," she cried, reaching out the window for it. He handed it to her, their eyes lingered, and she stepped on the starter. "Till tomorrow," she said, and looking back as she turned into the road she saw him still standing beside the steps looking after her. She was the first to wave.

I I

WHEN SHE REACHED HER ROOM AT THE
hotel, she put her red camellia in water in the bathroom
tumbler and set it on the bedside table. It was still fresh,
and glowed with a deep garnet color, richer than any rose
she had ever owned. Then she methodically washed out the
picnic bottles and set them to dry, and discarded all
the food in the tin box. In the morning she would get the
hotel people to make chicken sandwiches, she would buy
fresh cheese and crackers and fruit at the store, and some
packaged cake and cookies — a schoolgirl spread, childishly
lavish, to make him a picnic. One bottle of tea, and one of
coffee. A man might prefer coffee.

But this belated recollection of his maleness caused no
mental stumble in her happy anticipation of tomorrow. His
rather preoccupied courtesy, his gentle indifference towards
life itself, removed him from her limited preconceptions of
the masculine category, so that she felt no shyness and no
reservations about the day to come — only a friendly eagerness to see him again, and a secret, almost subconscious
excitement.

She got out her books and note-books and reread the bits about the headquarters at the house named for the Fountain — a brick house, substantial enough to act as a fort, said by later historians to have disappeared except for traces of the foundations. Less than half a mile behind where it had stood were the almost legendary springs — polished black water, said one of the older books, bubbling up from a creamy marl slope, to form a wide, quiet creek which flowed over a shady bed beneath moss-draped cypress trees, and disappeared again into a subterranean cavern. Once it had run red with the blood of wounded patriot soldiers who crawled there after the battle to drink at the source among the cypress knees, and dress their wounds beside the stream below. The British had been driven off that day, and the ground was held, but at what cost. And in the end it had to be abandoned anyway, so that the invaders in their turn quenched thirst at the source, bathed wounds in the dark, clear water. . . .

Mary sat dreaming in the hotel bedroom, with the books open on her lap. She had hardly hoped to find the Fountain, much less to see it with the perfect companion who was already familiar with its whereabouts and background. So Something had happened, after all. The General, she was sure, had a hand in this. The General was watching. It was because of him she had come to Fleetwood and the burying ground, and the last Creston, whose other name she did not know.

The next day was still warmer, a real foretaste of the

[23]

Carolina summer. When she turned the car in under the great live oaks which shaded Fleetwood, he was waiting on the steps with some books in his hands — those from his library which he thought might interest her. Among them was one with an old engraving of the Fountain, showing remnants of the house still standing in the distance. There was nothing left there now but a few broken bricks, he said, sitting beside her as they drove further into the wilderness. His own minute knowledge of her subject was unfolding slowly and with diffidence, till she cried that he ought to be writing a book himself, and he said no, that it was a pastime with him only, as it was with many other inhabitants of the district, which was full of half-forgotten history.

At his direction she took a sandy track leading off the road under sweet-gums, towering pines, and live oaks. The shade was so dense that there was little undergrowth, except for the glossy dark leaves of great magnolias and the golden gleam of wild yellow jessamine. Soon the track dipped to lower ground and ran beside a miniature cypress swamp where the trees stood tall and mysterious with their feet in the water which made a dark mirror to the sky and the great, motionless moss streamers which hung from the high branches. Filtered sunlight chiseled out the straight, colonnaded trunks in a strange vertical pattern of highlight and shadow reflected in magic duplicate on the still surface, till the eye was dizzied and confused.

What passed for a road simply came to an end on a low

bank running down to the verge, and when Mary stopped the car and shut off the engine the plash of falling water was audible in the sudden silence. "Oh!" she said softly, and sat a moment, just looking, before she moved to get out of the car.

Stepping out on his side then, he came round in front of the car and stood beside her, listening to the water, watching her childlike pleasure. He had known the Fountain all his life, and had visited it many times, usually alone. All those empty hours beside it — he was thinking, as they stood there — all leading up to this day, and this perfect companion, so simply enchanted, so without female guile, so perilously young and confiding in the stranger who was himself, so pathetically young, no matter what her actual age, and so soon to be lost again from the bleakness in which he lived. Someone ought to tell her, he was thinking, that she ought not to go about entrusting herself to people like this — she was safe today, indeed, but what about the next fellow, what about after she was gone from him again, who could guarantee that it would always be the right sort of person who volunteered to show her a hidden landmark? Who but the General, who had brought her here and would doubtless see her safe home again. . . .

"Oh, thank you!" said Mary, looking up at him, solemn in her joy and satisfaction — and then she caught the reflection of his thoughts in his face and her eyes lingered again in his, held by the kindness there, and something like compassion which she could not understand. How good he

[25]

is, went through her mind as she looked, and how comfortable it would be to have him in one's life, wise and patient and — always there. It's more than women, the revelation ran, the thing that there is in him. . . . "Thank you for coming here with me," she said, to break a silence that was becoming poignant. "One could never imagine anything like it. Are those what are called cypress knees in the water?"

"They are. The source is just out of sight around to the left, and there is a bank where I've often sat and watched the water. We could carry the books over there to look at them, if you like, and I want you to take home with you anything that might be of use."

"There's a rug in the back of the car to sit on — would it be sacrilege to eat our lunch here by the water?"

"If it is I've committed it many times myself," he smiled.

As they handled the books, sitting together on the plaid wool rug from the car laid on thick grass which was strewn with violets and yellow jessamine, and later as they ate the picnic lunch and he lighted a cigarette at the end of the meal, she noticed again the unsteadiness of his fine, long-fingered hands, in contrast to his unwavering eyes, and wondered vaguely again about drink, and brushed the idea away as unworthy.

There was more life in him today, and she developed an unusual talkativeness. Two hours passed in childlike, trivial conversation and easy companionship, and the sun had gone over and the shadows shifted to the east, and under the great trees it was suddenly almost twilight. There fell a little silence between them, the first, in which the water seemed to run more noisily. She began slowly to pack up the lunch things and tidy away the remains.

"Must you?" he asked, and his eyes rested on her face with an intimacy like a caressing hand.

"I suppose I must. I was due at the Museum today, and they'll be wondering what's become of me. I had a letter to a Mr. Morgan there from a man in Boston, which I sent on ahead, so I must turn up tomorrow morning. But it's been a wonderful day, I can never thank you enough for sharing it with me."

"I can't tell you what it's meant to me," he said simply.

They returned with reluctance to the car and drove back to Fleetwood, avoiding each other's eyes in a tardy self-conscious withdrawal from so sudden an attraction as they both inwardly acknowledged. When the car stopped in the driveway he stepped out at once and closed the door between them and stood looking in at her, his elbow on the lowered window.

"You'll send me a copy of the thesis when it's finished?" he asked wistfully.

"Oh, yes, I will. Wait, how do I return the books? Will you write down the address?" She handed him a note-book and pencil from the glove compartment, and sat watching his face while he wrote.

"That's not fair," he remarked as he handed back the paper. "I don't even know your name."

"I'm sorry! I somehow thought you did!" She seized the note-book and scribbled in it, tore out the page and gave it to him.

"Mary," he said, reading. "It's such a pretty name."

"I didn't realize you hadn't called me by it."

"May I?"

"Please do." She held out her hand to him, through the window. "Let's keep in touch. Will you write to me?"

He bent his head with unhurried ease and kissed her fingers in his.

"Thank you. Dear Mary," he said, and while their eyes still held, the car slid away.

There was nothing else to do, she told herself all the way back to the hotel, but say Good-bye. She had still no idea of his obligations or relationships, beyond the absent mother. It didn't seem possible he had told her so little about himself — she was by now an open book to him. Surely in all that time together, a wife would have been referred to if there was, or had been, a wife. She had been frank enough about her own unspoken-for status. Perhaps too frank? He seemed to take it for granted that she knew how he was placed.

She looked down at her right hand on the wheel, where his lips had rested. Such a graceful, unpremeditated gesture, the kiss had been. Nothing of the kind had ever happened to her before, she would not have believed that anybody would kiss a woman's hand these days, outside of Hollywood. But the kiss was real. Dear Mary, he said. Her heart

bumped a little, and was quiet again. If he didn't forget . . .

She realized with astonishment as she reached the hotel
that for the first time in her life she was dreaming about a
live man instead of a dead hero.

I I I

"Ridgeway Creston?" said Mr. Morgan at the Museum the next day, when she made a discreet inquiry after having craftily introduced the subject of the Sibley girls first. "Oh, Lord, yes — he probably knows all there is to know about this country. Used to have a very fine library at Fleetwood. Some of those old houses still have forgotten first editions of Pope and Defoe and so forth that have been on the shelves ever since they were first ordered from London as new publications. Some people live for years on the sale of their libraries to rare book dealers. Ridgeway Creston is a sad case, but not unusual down here."

"Sad?" A little tremor ran through her. "I didn't think — he seemed all right, I thought."

"You must have hit one of his good days," said Mr. Morgan. "Perhaps I shouldn't put it like that, though. Ridge never stood a chance. No man who has lived all his life alone with his mother does. Mrs. Creston is a — well, call it unbalanced. His father was killed by a horse a few days before Ridge was born, and she's never got over it. It wasn't enough for her to have the horse shot, she took her grief and loneliness out on the child, for some unknown reason — seemed to hate him, always, and he grew up hating her right back. His service in the Army might have saved him, but that seems to have gone wrong too — some dull, frustrating job in the Pacific which wrecked his health. Then while he was away the dam went in here, and they lost all but a few acres of the property — *she* made difficulties right and left, and put everybody's back up, and they lost heavily on the compensation they might have got. That was sort of the last straw for Ridge, I guess. When he came out of the service he just as good as resigned from the human race. Most of their neighbors are gone now, because of the dam. Most of the rest have died off. He and his mother live there together, in that big house, with a couple of ancient servants and nothing to keep it up."

"It's a beautiful house still." Mary could find nothing else to say. She felt embarrassed and guilty, hearing all this behind his back, as though she had pried into things he had not seen fit to tell her, but it had become impossible now to shut off the flow of Morgan's gossip without sounding abrupt and making him think twice, which was the last thing she wanted.

"There was a lot of money in the Creston family once," he rambled on. "Nobody knows where it came from, probably hers. His father met and married her in Kentucky, I believe — all before my time. And nobody knows what became of it after he died, but suddenly the place just began to run down. They sell off timber, of course, and probably

[31]

the books and antiques from the house, like all those old places. *She* had an expensive whim to wire the house for electricity and put in a bathroom and so on, when the dam went in. It was while Ridge was still away, and her sister was living there with her. But before he went into the Army he was at a good law school, and I think he had passed his Bar exams."

"Well, then — isn't he a lawyer?"

"He's never practiced law, as far as I know. Now he apparently sits around all day reading trash from the public library here in town, and drinking a bit too much when he has it. I met him on the street not long ago and got a shock — he had the shakes, and he looked hungry. I'm ashamed to say I found it hard to pass the time of day with him."

"But — what becomes of him?"

"Nothing, he just goes on. His mother will die one day, but that will be too late for Ridge, she's broken him. It's good blood, good brains, too, once. No hope for him now, of course."

"But that's dreadful." She felt rather sick.

"Yes, it is. But nobody can do anything about it, except Ridge himself, and he's past trying now."

"He — never married?" Morgan had told her so much, she might as well know that too.

"Never had much chance. She always kept him under her thumb, and what money there is she controls."

"How dreadful," she said again, almost unconscious that she spoke, and he glanced sharply at her.

"Did you see much of him, then?"

"No. Oh, no." She forced herself out of her reverie. "But he knew so well what I was talking about. He even lent me some of his books to take home. It seems a pity."

"He's not the only one of that generation to find himself at a loose end. Especially here in the South."

She saw the man's interest wandering, and with a few more remarks about the original reason for her visit she left him.

I V

Once headed northward again, she found herself hurrying. And instead of shaping whole paragraphs in her mind about the General, as she had done on the way down, she kept devising over and over again the brief, noncommittal letter she would write to accompany the borrowed books when she returned them — but a letter which would somehow leave an opening for a reply. . . .

When the heat and languor of the Southern countryside had given way to the crisp spring greenness of New England, she half expected the edge of her new preoccupation to dull a little with distance and the return to familiar surroundings. But the vivid memory of him was still there at her side when she arrived, late one afternoon, in front of the white dolls' house with green shutters and a close-mown lawn under shady elms that was home — the tidy, wholly feminine, almost spinsterish life she had stepped out of into a state of what she now acknowledged to be wholesale confusion.

She tried to see it with his eyes, as though she had never seen it before — the newly painted look, the disciplined bloom, the bright porch furniture — nothing worn, nothing run-down, nothing seedy-looking. For the first time it occurred to her to wonder what her mother's income was, and to notice the almost aggressive prosperity she had always taken for granted. And then she tried to see him with their eyes — and that was easier. His spare, leisurely body in the not quite fresh, rather limp white suit — his low, pleasant voice, with its lingering syllables that still did not constitute what was loosely called a drawl — his beautiful, unsteady hands, the perpetual cigarette, the lack of animation in his face — disinterest, rather than boredom, as though he had simply seceded from society. She had seen his face kindled and laughing, but that was the General's doing, he had made them friends. But surely no one, not even Aunt Lucy, could overlook his level, disturbing eyes. . . .

That evening after dinner she went up to her bedroom with its pink spread and white curtains and big mirrors and workmanlike writing-desk, and began to unpack her notebooks and papers and sort them out to line up her work for the next day. And then she sat down at the desk and took out the folded sheet of ruled paper on which he had written his address in a fine, spidery penmanship which showed no trace of the tremor in his hands. *Ridgeway Creston*. Very distinguished. But he said Mary was a pretty name. . . .

So he followed her even there, into her virgin room, so long chastely inhabited by the General who had been dead a hundred and seventy years. But Ridgeway Creston wasn't dead. At least, for a while that day at the Fountain he had forgotten to be. And the General had never kissed her hand.

She picked up a pen and wrote on a piece of foolscap: DEAR MR. CRESTON. No, not till she could return the books. Or perhaps — as soon as she had finished just one book, she had better return it singly, with a note. . . .

> Just to say that I have arrived home safely and found everything much the same [she wrote, experimentally, beneath the formal salutation]. Your books are here beside me on the desk, or I would almost think I had dreamed Fleetwood, and the Fountain. If the pictures I took come out well I will send you copies, but the light wasn't very good. I will get down to work tomorrow morning, and return your property as soon as I can. It was very good of you to trust me, a stranger, with such valuable material.
> Sincerely,
>
> MARY CARMICHAEL

Her chin stuck out a little as she sealed, addressed, and stamped the envelope. He had a right to know his books hadn't landed in a ditch somewhere. . . .

His reply when it came was bulky and several days overdue.

> DEAR MARY [he wrote]:
> You said I might!
> I was glad to learn of your safe arrival at home and to have proof — your letter — that I had not just recklessly imagined a girl named Mary who was everything I ever longed for but whom the Lord had never got round to

create. It was a tall order, but we are told that nothing is beyond Him, and now I know.

I have been to the Museum and found, as I suspected, that that silly fool Morgan never showed you the Pemberton letters. He says he got to talking — about what, for heaven's sake! — and forgot them. I made him get them out and I reread them, and copied a few pages (enclosed) which seemed to bear on your subject. If you want the whole lot copied I would be glad to do it, provided you can read what I've written, but I haven't got a typewriter. There are about twenty altogether, some long, some short, all written after the Yorktown surrender.

Please don't hesitate to let me know if I can be of any possible further use to you.

Faithfully yours,

RIDGE

She read it three times, unbelieving. Then she read the letters he had copied — four closely written pages in his difficult, spidery handwriting. She couldn't possibly ask for more. And yet — mightn't it be good for him to have it to do, to be encouraged to go to the Museum and resume contacts with people like Morgan — *bless* the man Morgan, anyhow — it must be very carefully done, of course — perhaps if she asked if there were any actual references to Yorktown in the letters, and wanted those copied down, as a starter . . . At least, it was necessary to answer at once. But how to deal with his first paragraph — one couldn't just ignore it, as he had done once he had written it — and yet, what else could one do . . . *Faith-*

[37]

fully yours. It was like his handwriting — like the kiss on her fingers — all eighteenth-century and astonishing.

DEAR RIDGE, she wrote, and sat looking at the paper a long time. That opening paragraph of his. It's my first love letter, she thought absurdly, and blushed, alone in her room. Well, perhaps it isn't quite a love letter, but — perhaps it's just a gesture, really, like kissing my hand — Southern men are supposed to be like that — I mustn't be New England and naïve. He probably wouldn't have done it if he hadn't been sure he'd never see me again. . . .

Feeling very sensible and tactful, then, she evolved a brief, friendly letter thanking him for the enclosure and inquiring about the Yorktown references. And when that was sealed and stamped, she laid her lips to his opening paragraph in gratitude and humility, and with a physical shock received a distinct impression of cigarette smoke.

Having begun, the letters went on. His continued to be bewilderingly defenceless and intimate — he was apparently quite content to lyricize and eventually openly to worship from a distance, in hopeless, uncomplaining acceptance of the fact that she had only passed by, and would not come that way again.

But her own mind began to query timidly. Does it end here? Is this meant to be all? He was not the kind of man she could ever fall in love with. For one thing, her staunch New England traditions insisted that a man who *was* a man had a job — went out and *got* a job — *did* something — *earned* something — *was* something. And at the same time her sixth sense warned her that in the rural South things were different for men like Ridge. There weren't the same opportunities nor the same incentives, and there were mysterious taboos. She didn't understand the difference, but she knew there was one. The fact remained that he was the opposite of everything she had ever dreamed of, in a man.

And what about his mother, who must have returned home by now, and who was said by the man Morgan to be unbalanced? Mary had not forgotten the terrible words, so casually spoken — *took her grief and loneliness out on the child . . . seemed to hate him, always, and he grew up hating her right back.* To Mary, so lavishly loved from babyhood, the idea always brought a shiver. To live like that, to sit at table, to make conversation, perhaps even to try to laugh — for presumably they must make some pretence of a daily existence together — with a person you did not like, discounting the stronger word Morgan had used — that would account for almost anything, wouldn't it, even the aimless idleness, even the matter-of-fact readiness for the peace and stillness of the grave, even — if it was so — the drink. No love? she wondered more than once, wincing for him. No love even as a child? And furthermore, no — romance, as she had none?

Nevertheless, his passive acceptance of the dead-end situation was evidence of the characteristics in him which she most deplored. Even his appearance — she could not imagine him wearing anything but a rather mussed white suit

— not a man to introduce with pride into her own critical circle as a . . . well, a fiancé! And for herself to enter the death-in-life that was his own existence? No one, however much infatuated, could contemplate that. Besides — she could never marry a man with a weakness for drink. Blast the Morgan man. Or was it only gossip, that Ridge drank? As things were between them now, he would tell her the truth about that if she chose to ask him.

The necessity to go back and see him again began to grow on her, though she wondered if perhaps he would rather that she didn't, now — if he would prefer to go on in his chosen half-world of twilit passion, where the realities of mere subsistence could not intrude. She had that bit of money of her own, but she could not touch the capital. Her mother might be willing to give her more, but she had no idea if there would be enough for that in her mother's portion. Besides — no man would live on his wife's money.

Meanwhile the normal, inevitable trend of her daily life continued. The thesis was duly finished, without any spectacular revelations to make it anything more than a very competent piece of work. It was accepted, and she received her M.A. with appropriate ceremonies, and the interviews for her first teaching job began. One took her to New York — Aunt Lucy went along, to see some plays. One took her to Boston — then it was her mother's turn to go along. There was no opening at her own college, to permit her to go on living at home, as she had done all through her uneventful off-campus college career, and her departure from the nest was again a source of perpetual discussion and dismay to her mother and her aunt. What more could they say, she began to wonder, when she broke it to them that first she was going South again, to see Ridge?

It simply never occurred to anyone else that she would hesitate over so flattering an opportunity as Merriwether Women's College, outside Boston, now offered, until she found herself sitting in the President's office hearing talk about signing a contract to teach there — with the guilty intention to go back to South Carolina *first* looking over her shoulder. A *contract*. She felt them waiting, and met the serene but questioning gaze of the President of the College and the Head of the History Department. They were perhaps prepared for some minor question of dates or transportation. She rose in a single movement as though for flight, gripped by a tightness in the throat, a swift panic — a hunch?

"I'm sorry," she said, to their unconcealed surprise. "I — could you give me a few more days — as much as a week?"

They glanced at each other. It was already an emergency, caused by a sudden death in the faculty, which had caught them with the post empty so late in the summer. She had seemed the sensible type. No love affairs, surely. Healthy. Nothing wrong with the money, as they well knew. What then?

"It's — a case of stage-fright, I guess," she stammered,

and her knuckles were white against the edge of the table. "It looks awfully big — all of a sudden. Would you let me go home and think it over for a few days? I'll wire you at once, when I decide."

They could not approve, but she was much the best they had seen, and they felt reasonably sure that she would settle down to it. Smiling indulgently, for it was indeed a responsible post for a beginner, they allowed her a week. No more. They would hold it open until they heard from her by wire, for one week.

She escaped from the office into the summer afternoon and walked rather blindly down the unfamiliar street of the quiet college town. It was already August, and they had granted her an enormous favor in the delay. She was really as bound by it as though she had signed the contract, and it would be very damaging not to go through with it now if she ever expected to teach anywhere. Teaching was what she had been trained to do, in order to be self-supporting, as her progressive-minded if totally unemployed female family believed a girl should be nowadays. But she could not combine teaching at Merriwether College — or anywhere else for that matter — with being Ridge's wife in Ridge's house. He had never asked her to be his wife. He probably never would. And yet — she must go back. Difficult to explain to her own people. Still more difficult, perhaps, to explain to him. He had written those letters on the fatalistic assumption that they would never meet again in this life. He might be embarrassed —

horrified, even — at the idea of facing her now. But — she had to go back. At once.

A letter from him was awaiting her when she got home. This, she told herself rationally, is the hunch. Something held me back from signing. Something laid a hand on my arm. When I read this, I'll know what it was. . . .

MY DARLING [Ridge had written recklessly]:

Does anyone else read my letters to you? Does anyone look over your shoulder as you write to me? Does the Puritan air of Massachusetts restrain you? Or is it just that you are afraid of too much love, even at this distance? Because your dear little letters all wear prim little pinafores of discretion and understatement, except now and then a sentence which escapes you and sets my heart on fire. And those are the ones I live for.

Your letters to me are quite safe here, you know. Because when I have learned them by heart, and I do, I kiss them good-bye and burn them, just in case I should meet with a sudden end and some other eye but mine should fall on them.

You say I am not wise to lay so much devotion at the feet of so brief a friendship as ours. Is it friendship that makes me start each day with the secret knowledge of you coming up inside me like a second sunrise? And is it friendship that I ache with in the long white nights? Why should I be wise about you? And what have mere counted hours to do with you and me? Forgive all these rhetorical questions. We were together, all told, for hardly the space of a single summer afternoon, but you left me a memory to cherish like a wife. . . .

Mary put that letter in her pocket, held tight to it, and went downstairs. The two good, innocent women who until now had always known every furthest corner of her schoolgirl existence were puzzled, incredulous, and then tearful, when she told them what she was going to do. It was like the first time she had set out for the South, only much worse. They had noticed his letters, of course — their frequency, their bulk, and the fact that she read them upstairs in her room. She said they were from a man she had met who was doing some copying for her at the Museum, just out of kindness. Finally, when the thesis was finished, and their curiosity outgrew her explanations, she had taken to trying to intercept the postman.

Now when they asked her who he was, she could only say that he came of a very good family which had once been well off, and lived with his mother, who wasn't well. They asked what he did and what his prospects were, and she had to say that he did nothing and hadn't had any prospects since he came out of the Army. They asked what she meant to do about the job at Merriwether College, and she replied that she couldn't tell — yet. They asked what she expected to live on if she married him, and she had to admit that she didn't know. They asked if he had proposed to her by letter, and she answered that he had not. They wanted to know what made her think he would propose if she went back, and she couldn't explain. They tried to extract from her a promise that she wouldn't marry this creature until they had seen him, and she refused. It was really a horrible scene.

She fled from it to her room, where her bag had not yet been unpacked. She exchanged some of its more formal contents for cool cotton and nylon frocks — August in Carolina — and drove away the following morning very early, with no more luggage in the car than she had taken with her the first time, except for two of his books. Life in the little white dolls' house had now become insupportable, and if she was not going to sign up with Merriwether College she must let them know within a week and they were going to be very annoyed.

V

SHE GAVE HIM NO WARNING THAT SHE WAS
coming, for fear he might do something quixotic. She
wanted to see his face, taken by surprise, and read in it
whatever his good manners or kind heart might have en-
abled him to conceal from her if he had time to think.
This meant also that at least one of his letters might arrive
after she had gone, and she wondered what Aunt Lucy and
her mother would make of it if in their outraged, thwarted
monopoly of their only chick they considered themselves
justified in opening and reading it. At least they would
learn that he was literate.

She reached the Virginia border the first night — a gruel-
ling drive, but she had liked the hotel on the way up and
sped back to it now with a sense of homing. She fell into
bed and slept, too tired even to dream. In the morning she
pressed on again, covering almost twice the ground she
had allotted to a day's driving before. And it was hot —
the lowland heat, humid, enervating, relentless, in which
the tightly buttoned British army had once succumbed by
the dozens to sheer exhaustion, while her General's spare,

tough fighting men, nearly naked from necessity, were able to endure.

On the afternoon of the third day she arrived, stiff, hungry, exhausted, and beginning to be frightened, at the little hotel in South Carolina from which she had set out — how many light-years ago! — to ·find the site of a vanished church and a legendary burying ground.

Everyone remembered her at once and was delighted to have her back again. She had a late lunch and a quick bath and rested a few minutes on the bed. By now her own hands were trembling and her hasty lunch — too near the bath — was not sitting well. Her eyes looked back at her from the mirror, very bright, but shadowed. You look scared to death, she told her image, and so you should be.

As she picked up her key to leave the room she paused, her hand on the inner knob, and took a deep breath. Before she stood inside that door again, on her return, her whole life would have changed. One way or another, when she walked out of that room she left the old Mary Carmichael behind. Even if it wasn't the future Mary Creston who came back to it — Mary Carmichael would never be the same. You don't have to, something inside her suggested. Yes, I do, she replied to it firmly, and opened the door.

Moving as it were outside herself, guided as it were by the General's firm, adventurous hand rather than her own volition, she went down to the dining-room and collected the picnic kit, which she had left to be filled with tea and sandwiches, and stopped again at the grocery store for a bag of fruit and packaged cake. Then she collected the car, which had been serviced at the garage across the street.

"Looks like we're in for a storm," said the boy in the monkey suit as she paid the bill, and she glanced vaguely at the sky, which had become overcast since she had last noticed it, and she sniffed the hot muggy air.

"Do us good," she said. "I hate them, though."

With a shrug, the boy watched her drive out towards it.

Fleetwood was still there. She suppressed a last-minute panic which nearly shot her past it, and pulled up in the drive below the steps. No one came to meet her. This was a crazy thing to do, she told herself too late. I should have let him know.

She knocked, and there was a step within — not Ridge's. A woman was crossing the hall.

"Good afternoon," said Mary through the screen. "Are you Mrs. Creston? I'm — "

As she spoke there was a flurry of feet on the stairs, a streak of white, and Ridge was at the door.

"I saw the car — it can't be — *Mary!*"

"I've brought back the last of your books," she said. "It seemed safer than mailing them."

He opened the screen and his hands drew her over the threshold — both his hands. It was all there, in his face — the welcome, the worship, the laughter, the tenderness.

"But I had a letter from you only yesterday — or was it the day before?" he was saying.

"I left very suddenly, and travelled very fast."

"With wings, I should think!"

His mother stood watching them, in the middle of the hall — unsmiling, hostile with surprise, already resenting the delay in acknowledging her presence. He turned to her, releasing Mary's hands.

"This is Mary Carmichael," he said. That was all. Obviously he had never told her who Mary Carmichael was. "My mother, Mary."

"How do you do?" said Mary, and put out a friendly little hand.

For a moment she wondered if the routine civilities were going to be completely ignored. Belatedly and briefly, Mrs. Creston accepted her hand, without comment.

"I probably shouldn't have come charging out here like this," Mary went on, feeling like a forward child. "But I wanted to go on to the Fountain for tea, if there's time."

"Today?" said Ridge, with noticeable hesitation.

"Yes, please, I've got the picnic things in the car. I — I'm supposed to get some more pictures. The others weren't any good."

The excuse, the story she had prepared for Mrs. Creston's benefit, came out rather lamely before the woman's immobility, the hard, black eyes which had never left her face, the effect of contemptuous suspicion which surrounded her like an aura. She was dark and gaunt and wooden. There was nothing of Ridge visible in her, he must be entirely his father's son. Screwed to the breaking-point anyway,

[49]

Mary felt the panic surge within her again, knew that she must get Ridge away quickly, out of the house, out of the malignant presence, or crumple abjectly before it with her mission in ruins.

"An illustrated magazine is taking an interest in the General's story, and wants pictures to go with an article based on my thesis," she explained elaborately, and wondered if it sounded like sheer babbling to them too. "I've got a better camera now, and have to try again. Will you come with me, Ridge?"

"You'll run into this storm if you go to the Fountain now," said Mrs. Creston.

"Please, Ridge — "

"We'll chance it," he said, opening the door. "Come on."

She ran down the steps ahead of him and jumped into the car. The storm was definitely lowering, but she took no notice of it. Before Ridge had closed the car door behind him they were in motion, out into the road which led to the Fountain.

"Sorry," she said tersely. "I didn't handle that very well, did I?"

As soon as they were out of sight of the house he took her right hand from the wheel and laid his lips against it — an odd, gentle, muted gesture of thanksgiving and defeat. And she said, her eyes on the road — "There isn't any magazine article. I made that up. I came back because I had to."

There was a long silence in the car.

"I could just manage to get along when I thought I'd

never see you again," he said. "Now I won't be able to bear it at all."

"We'll bear it together," she said confidently, and he raised his head to look at her.

"You — can't mean you'd *stay* here!"

"I could," she said, with a swift recklessness which took her own breath away, for now she knew, without any doubt, how he felt, off guard, at sight of her again.

"But — you saw Morgan at the Museum. Don't tell me he didn't gossip like an old woman! You must have heard from him that I'm no good, and there's no money, and how my life is. I can't — couldn't ask anyone to marry me."

"I can't argue with you and drive at the same time," she said gently. "Wait till we get to the Fountain."

"Are you going to argue with me?" he asked hopefully, and she nodded, and he was obediently silent.

The car made the sharp turn into the sandy track which wound beneath the hanging moss. Because of the oncoming storm the light was sulphurous and queer, and the muggy heat lay against their faces like a damp veil. As she pulled up beside the stream and cut off the engine she realized belatedly that the spot was an invitation to lovers in parked cars, and at the same moment his arms closed round her, drawing her gently from under the wheel and up against him. His first kiss was quiet, almost compassionate, and she rested against his shoulder, her face upturned to his, while he touched her hair and cheek with trembling fingers.

"It's not possible," he whispered. "I don't believe it's happening. I shall wake up soon and you won't be here."

"It didn't feel like a dream," she told him honestly. "Nobody's ever done that before."

His hand under her chin was kind and undemanding. She nestled to it like a puppy, and saw his eyes flare up with something more than amusement. His next kiss was more urgent, and the next, but still there was a quality of renunciation, as though each time their lips parted for a few murmured words it would be the last time ever. She accepted his lovemaking with perfect confidence, and he took fire from her unpracticed response, until with a noticeable effort he released her, kissed both her hands and gave them back to her, and stumbled out of the car, feeling for his cigarettes.

From the seat she watched him strike two matches before his cigarette caught, while the sound of falling water filled the silence between them. Then he turned, holding the door open for her, so that she too got out of the car and they walked hand in hand to the bank and sat down together on a ledge above the source.

For a moment he smoked, withdrawn and self-contained, almost as though she was not there, and a low rumble of thunder could be heard in the distance. The yellow, murky light seemed very nearly to have substance and texture in the unnatural heat, and there was nothing of the sun in its color.

"It *is* going to storm," she said, and her voice sounded

small and uncertain on the commonplace words above the sobbing bubble of the spring, and he nodded.

"We mustn't stay here long," he said, without making a move to go. "We must talk, and then get you back to the hotel before the storm breaks, it's overdue. I'm only trying to think what I must say to you now."

"I wonder what the General thinks," she smiled, with an affectionate glance round at what seemed still the General's territory.

"I know very well what he thinks. He would never have got out of the car when I did!"

She laid her cheek against the end of his shoulder, with her fingers laced in his — a gesture of confiding contentment which closed his hand in quick, hard gratitude.

"You didn't try to stop me in the car," he said, marvelling. "You weren't afraid of me. But you ought to *know* enough to be afraid!"

"Of you?" She laughed comfortably, and kissed his sleeve at the shoulder, and laid her cheek on the spot again.

"I might suggest for your future good," he said with deliberate pedantry, "that it's not wise to give just anybody the opportunities I had just now."

Her laughter was free and spontaneous.

"Darling, you needn't sound so stuffy! I don't go round kissing men in cars! Nobody ever wanted me to before!"

"Massachusetts must be a very backward sort of place."

"Oh, I'm just the mousy kind that nobody notices," she confessed cheerfully.

[53]

He saw that she was quite ready for another kiss, and again released her with an effort, tossed his cigarette to the sandy ground at their feet and rose to set his heel on it. Then with both hands firmly in his pockets, he stood facing her while thunder rumbled nearer above the sound of the spring.

"We're going to get a howling storm," he said. "There isn't much time before we must get out of here. My darling — nothing could be more wonderful than to have you come back to me like this, but you must see for yourself that it leads to nothing — can't you? I'm done for, there's nothing left here, I've nothing to offer a woman — "

"You were doing all right in the car," she said, with one of the bright, sidelong glances which came so oddly from her usual innocent gravity.

He faltered before its implications, wavered towards her, and restrained himself. The thunder was much louder, and the light was turning a muddier yellow.

"You've really thought seriously about — about marrying me?" he asked.

"We-ell — " She looked down, plaiting her fingers in her lap with a new, intentional coquetry. "I haven't rightly speaking been asked to."

He dropped to one knee beside the ledge where she sat, which brought him to the level where he could lay his arms around her.

"Seriously, I said," he insisted. "You must see that I can't ask anybody to come and live at Fleetwood, as things

[54]

are. It's my mother's home, and no woman, that is, no wife of mine, could put up with her, there's no getting round that. She's — a little off, you know. What's more, I'm supposed to be a little off, myself."

"Well, look at me, I'm crazier than any of you, I came back here and asked for it!" she pointed out, and he caught her to him, burying his face against her breast, and she held him there, laughing because she was so sure that they could find a solution between them. But something in his stillness became ominous, and she bent over him, raising his head between her hands. To her dismay, his eyes were blurred with tears.

"You're making it very difficult for me to do the right thing," he said unsteadily, and *"Darling*, we'll find a way, there's always a way when people are in love!" she cried in her touching ignorance, and kissed his face, on the cheekbone, and then lightly on the lips. He let her, without moving or responding. "We can't lose each other now," she went on, trying to speak confidently in the face of his inertia. "Think of the General! There must have been lots of times when he couldn't see his way — no guns, no horses, no food, not enough men — but he always came out swinging. He may have lost the battles, but he won the war! He must have stood on this very spot, feeling beaten and sick of life, but he went on *trying*. Ridge, how can you dare to give up before we even try!"

He looked up at her from his knees beside the ledge, leaning on her lap.

[55]

"I think he usually knew the odds," he said. "Perhaps if I could once take this in and *believe* it, I could get a grip on things. Tell me again — help me to understand — did you come back here to marry me?"

"Are you asking me to?"

"Yes — no — I *mustn't*, not yet, not till there's some sort of life for you to live here! I must think, and I haven't thought in years. I'll have to learn to think all over again, and for somebody else. You see, for the first time it *matters* now. Because of you. I thought I was dead and buried, and I didn't care any more, and now you make me feel things again — *want* things. You must make me think, next."

"That's harder," she said, smiling, and his eyes, no longer doglike, no longer blinded by tears, but quick and caressing, ran over her face again.

"*Why?*" he said urgently — the old, old question between lovers. "Tell me why. I'm too old for you. I have bad times, you know that, don't you — worse times, I mean, when I'm not fit — "

"That's not thinking, that's just talking out loud," she warned him. "There won't be any bad times, when we're together. There won't be time for them, we'll be too busy — "

Lightning flashed, and a crack of thunder came close upon it, and rumbled away. High up in the tops of the great cypress trees a small wind was rising, yet the moss just above their heads hung motionless and the heavy air they breathed did not stir.

"We must go," he said, and she laid her arms around his shoulders before he could rise from beside her.

"You still haven't asked me to marry you," she reminded him. "Maybe you'd rather not, in any case. I don't want to take too much for granted."

"I would rather marry you tomorrow than go to heaven when I die," he said solemnly. "But — "

She laid her fingers on his lips.

"That's all I want to know now," she said, on another burst of thunder and lightning, and the first raindrops began to fall, dimpling the dark surface of the water.

"We'll have to run for it." He rose quickly. "I'll go ahead and get the door open."

They pelted to the car and landed breathless and laughing on the seat and rolled up the windows.

"I hate thunderstorms," she confessed. "Shall we go back to Fleetwood and unpack our tea and have a picnic there anyhow, with your mother?"

"I think it would be better to go straight to the hotel, if we can make it."

"But it's farther than the house. And I want to know her."

"We may have no choice," he conceded, as lightning ripped across the sky in front of them and she put the car in motion, and the noise of the engine did not cover the deafening roll of thunder which followed. "I should have got you out of this sooner."

"They always say you're perfectly safe in a car in a thunderstorm," she said bravely.

[57]

"You are."

"But all the same, I'd rather be in a building."

She drove steadily, trying not to wince at each flash, peering ahead into blinding sheets of rain while the windshield wiper worked furiously.

"This is going to be a bad one, it's been gathering for days," he said after a few minutes. "We can never get into town through this. But if you've any ideas of winning my mother over in an afternoon you're in for a shock."

"We'll take the tea things in, that will help. It's got so dark, I'd better put the lights on."

"It's nearer dinner time than tea time, anyway. You won't — mind anything she says, will you?"

"What sort of thing is she likely to say?"

"One never knows. She likes to turn your own words back on you, with a different meaning. But don't be drawn. Don't answer back. The best way is not to answer at all."

"Don't forget, I live with a couple of pretty cranky old women myself," she reminded him. "Sometimes I think they *try* to pick a fight."

"I'm afraid you've still got a lot to learn about that."

"Don't worry, Ridge, we can handle it. After all, it's not just a social call, it's forced on us. I'd be terrified to try to get as far as the hotel in this. You don't seem to mind it at all."

"We get these equinoctial storms each year."

"Now, that," she said with emphasis, "is the first real drawback I've heard!"

[58]

"You're awfully funny," he said softly against the noise of the storm, "and awfully sweet — and I adore you."

"Then I don't mind anything, even thunder and lightning," she was saying when a new blast forced a startled "*Oh!*" from her and the car swerved and righted itself.

"Steady, we're almost there. Have you got a coat? You'll be soaked getting as far as the porch."

"My raincoat's in the back seat. I thought we might get a shower! What about you?"

"I'll be all right."

She stopped the car at the foot of the steps and he helped her into the coat, which had a hood attached.

"You take the picnic kit and open the door and run," she said. "Don't wait for me, I'm covered."

She reached the shelter of the porch only seconds behind him, carrying the rest of the food, and they stood a moment looking back into the storm. It had got quite dark, and the wind had risen wildly.

"It will go on like this all night now," he said calmly, and she hunched her shoulders in a childish gesture of uneasiness.

"Then may I please stay here with you till it stops? Will you *please* sit up with me, and keep the lights on, till it's over?"

"There's no choice," he said again, and held open the screen door for her to enter the house.

V I

A LIGHTED LAMP WITH A RATHER WEAK bulb under a thick shade stood on a small table in the entrance hall, throwing cavernous shadows into the corners and up the broad staircase. There was light in the room on the left beyond, and he guided her towards it, the picnic kit still in his hand.

The white-walled parlor was vast and dim, with the constant flare of the lightning outside long, uncurtained windows. There was only one lamp, and it had a large opaque shade, so that the light fell downward on the magnificent mahogany table in the middle of the room. In an armchair beside it Mrs. Creston sat with a large square of needle-point in her hands.

"It's impossible for Miss Carmichael to get back to the hotel in this weather," Ridge said as they entered. "It's ruined our picnic, so she suggested we have it here."

"A sort of high tea now, instead of dinner," Mary added with her disarming friendliness, as he set the kit down and helped her out of the raincoat. Because it was natural for her to notice such things, having herself been taught all kinds of needlework at a very tender age, she cast an interested glance at the piece Mrs. Creston was at work on. She had before now made friends with innumerable old ladies by asking them to show her how to do their stitch or pattern, even if she already knew it, and she hoped to establish common ground the same way with Ridge's mother. "I don't want to put you to any trouble, and everything is here, plenty for all three of us, I think."

"I have already had something to eat, thank you," said Mrs. Creston distantly, without raising her eyes from the cloth into which her needle dug and dug, viciously. "I hardly expected to see Ridge back tonight."

Mary's eyes widened, and she decided hastily that it couldn't have been meant the way it sounded. She glanced at Ridge, who had busied himself on the other side of the table with the picnic materials, and would not look up. He had taken out the sandwich box and laid it on the table, and she moved to his side to open it.

"May we just lay it out here?" she asked. "Perhaps you'll have a cup of tea with us anyway."

Mrs. Creston did not reply. The noise of the storm conveniently made conversation difficult, and it was a relief to Mary to occupy herself with setting out the simple meal. She turned her back on the windows and kept her eyes down, wishing for more light in the room to conceal the lightning flares, which seemed to be getting worse instead of passing over, and she had never known a thunderstorm of such violence to last so long.

"Up where I come from," she said, trying bravely to break the tension in the room, "a storm just comes and goes. Can it really keep this up for hours?"

"It usually does, once it gets started," Ridge said. "Something a little stronger than tea might help you to put up with it. There's a bottle of sherry, I think. I'll fetch it."

He disappeared into the unlighted regions beyond the hall, and Mary was left alone with the silent, hostile figure beside the lamp.

"I'm sorry to intrude like this, I hope you'll forgive me for inviting myself to stay," she said placatingly. "But I'm rather a fool about storms and I asked Ridge to stand by me till it stops. At home we always put on all the lights and get something to eat out of the ice-box if there's a storm at night, being just three women alone in the house."

"No man I've ever seen was any protection against a bolt of lightning," said Mrs. Creston above her needlework. "Of course it flatters them to have a woman like you behave as though they were."

"Well, I — " Mary could find no reply. It left her speechless with resentment of its swift implication, residing in ironic inflection even more than in words, that she was setting her cap at Ridge in all the obvious, cheap little ways to which she had never in her life given a thought. It left her feeling like a fluttery girl putting on an act to win attention from condescending males.

"The best way," Mrs. Creston was saying in her flat, harsh voice, so different from Ridge's caressing tones, "is just to go to bed — with or without a man — and forget about it."

Mary decided to treat that one as intentional humor instead of insult, and gave an uneasy little laugh.

"I suppose if you're strong-minded enough you can," she said. "But the next best thing is to make a cheerful noise with dishes and chatter."

"If you can get Ridge to make a cheerful noise," said Mrs. Creston. "He's not famous for it."

"Perhaps he's not had enough encouragement," said Mary directly, flinging down a gage of her own.

"He knows more about the other thing, certainly," said his mother, again with so much implied in the tone that Mary was again speechless, this time on Ridge's behalf. *Don't answer*, he had warned her. *She could always turn your words against you*, like a boomerang. *She does hate him*, Morgan knew what he was talking about, Mary thought incredulously. *I supposed he was using a figure of speech, but this is* — something queer and dreadful. *Why, when he's all she's got left? If she loved his father so much — so insanely*, Mary thought, groping through dark mysteries — *so that she can't bear it to have only Ridge left instead — Ridge must remind her, every move he makes, he must be his father's image — but she would have to be quite mad to hate him for that — unbalanced? — she's* mad — *unless, of course, she hated his father too*. . . .

Ridge returned, carrying a bottle half full of sherry, and a bouquet of stemmed glasses in his other hand.

"I left a light in the bathroom at the top of the stairs," he said. "In case you'd like to go up and wash before you eat."

"Thank you," she murmured, and escaped from the room, her head down, avoiding his eyes for fear the pity and horror she felt would show in her own. Ridge was living in a nightmare here. And no mention of his daily ordeal had escaped him, even in his letters, until he was forced by circumstances today to warn her that she would find his mother difficult. That alone took fortitude. And pride. She wished there were some way to protect his pride from her knowledge of what he had tried to conceal from her. She wished there were some way she could spare him even now from the rest of the evening and whatever it might bring of further revelation and embarrassment.

Ridge brought the glasses to the table and set them down carefully. He saw at a glance that something had been said to upset Mary, but there had been no way to offer her the hospitality of the bathroom without leaving them alone together.

"There's no need to insult her," he said quietly, determined not to be drawn, at least while Mary was in the house. "We probably won't see her again after tonight."

"One of your failures?" she asked with satisfaction.

With an effort, Ridge held back the first reply which occurred to him. It was one of his mother's obsessions that he was the same kind of wilful philanderer his father was supposed to have been — small wonder, he had often thought, if his father had strayed in search of warmth and laughter and a sunny face. Like Mary's, he thought, with a cramp at his heart. Why couldn't more women understand that the way to be loved was to be loving? His father had become in his mother's twisted mind a monster of infidelity, and his father's son was believed by her to have inherited his nature along with his looks. From Ridge's early boyhood she had accused him, if only by implication, of excesses which had long ago ceased to shock or anger him. And then, because she was never able to trace any young indiscretions on his part, and he never seemed to involve himself in scrapes to which she could point with triumph, and finally because he did not seem to think of marriage, and how could he, she had perversely begun to imply that he was lacking in manhood, as though to jockey him into alternate action if only to demonstrate. He was used to it, he seldom bothered to reply or defend himself, because it didn't matter enough. But now there was Mary. Now it mattered. The neck of the sherry bottle chattered against the rim of the glass as he poured, and he said in rare retaliation, "God knows I've been given no such reason to think well of women, or wish to add another one to my life."

"Are you sure you'd know what to do about it if she was willing?"

"Make up your mind!" he said savagely, without raising his voice, setting down the bottle with a thud. "Am I a Don Juan or — " Thunder drowned the rest of it.

When Mary re-entered the room he was standing at the window watching the storm. His mother appeared not to have moved, except for her stabbing needle. Three glasses of sherry waited in a golden group by the bottle.

He turned and came towards the light, angry and ashamed as though Mary had overheard, and now she was able to look at him mutely in reassurance and understanding. He handed her a glass, set one on the edge of the table beside his mother, who ignored it, and lifted his own to Mary.

"God bless you," he said gently, and drank. She echoed the toast, and after the first swallow said, "That's lovely, I'm sure to feel better soon! It's not letting up, is it!"

"Not yet. Aren't you getting used to it?" His eyes were humorous and kind, all the shadows banished from his face as he looked down at her.

"There was the most awful crash just as I got to the top of the stairs. It was all I could do not to *fling* myself down here yelling for you to save me!" she admitted comically, able to make fun of her own quite genuine fear.

"Drink up," he said sympathetically. "Dutch courage." And he refilled his own glass and waited for hers to be emptied.

They ate the sandwiches, drank the tea, and went on to the fruit and grocery-store cake, making determined conversation against the storm and the haughty silence on the other side of the table. There was a strange intimacy in the meal, rather than otherwise. They stood together against the elements and a mutual human enemy, and it was a certain challenge to behave to each other as though neither disturbance existed. When their eyes met, with laughter and open affection, they knew that she saw, and each glance they exchanged felt as revealing as a kiss, and yet it was their pride not to acknowledge self-consciousness or constraint. Each played up to the other, each respected and supported the other's gallant effort, until the eerie meal was finished and he lighted a cigarette.

She was convinced by now that he was truly not nervous of the storm. For him it actually did not matter, as a possible source of danger, he was able to dismiss it as a natural cataclysm to be sat through without apprehension. And yet there was no hint of ridicule in his acceptance of her own struggle against a growing terror of its violence. The wind was gale force now, howling in the chimney, beating at the windows, banging the blinds, striking the house with gusts which the whole structure seemed to feel in its very skeleton.

"I — suppose the house couldn't just blow in on us, could it?" she asked, suddenly unable to keep up the pretence that there was no storm.

"Well, it never has yet," he reminded her gently, as though entertaining the possibility out of mere politeness. "And it's stood here quite a while, and seen a good many nights like this. I hate you to be so frightened, a storm is really a very beautiful thing, you know. Lightning is an illumination we seldom see things by. It gives a completely

[67]

different perspective. Come and look." He rose, with a protective arm held out to her, and when she joined him unwillingly he drew her against his side and led her to the long window which faced the drive.

"The poor car!" she said. "Will it ever start again?"

"I hope so, mine is out of order," he said ruefully. "The garage promised to have it ready by the end of the week, but that's not much good, is it!"

"I suppose if the worst happens I could phone the hotel to send something to take me off your hands."

"You could, only there's no telephone."

"Oh, dear. Well, maybe you're just stuck with me," she said comfortably, and then a sheet of flame seemed to blot out the world, there was a crack and a splintering crash which shook the house, and in the shimmering aftermath a great tree split and fell across the yard, missing the house by less than its own length.

With a wordless sound of terror and apology, she hid her face against his coat, and felt his arm tighten while his other hand closed warm and comforting on hers, as he turned her away from the window.

"I didn't think it was so near," he said. "The worst will be over now. Come and sit down, that was a nasty one."

"Haven't you any nerves at all?" she gasped, for though he had instantly held her closer it was not a start of fear that had jerked his arm.

"Masses of nerves," he assured her truly. "But not that kind, I suppose."

[68]

"You weren't frightened," she insisted incredulously, and he put her into a chair and detached her clinging hands with a smile, and held out to her his crumpled pack of cigarettes.

"Have one of these," he said. "It gives you something to do."

There were only three left, and she shook her head.

"No, thanks, really. I'm all right now, and I just don't like the taste of them. I've tried."

"Do you mind . . . ?"

"Of course not. I'm sorry to be so silly, but I never saw a storm like this before. Suppose that tree had come this way and hit the roof!"

"We'd have had rather a wet night, I expect." He glanced at his mother unwillingly, and she met his eyes in defiance, refusing to speak the words he was waiting for. "You will certainly have to stay here until morning, though," he said after a moment. "There will be more trees down across the roads, and wires down too, probably. You must be tired, would you like to go to bed?"

"Oh, no, I'm much too nervous to sleep and I'd hate to be alone. Please let me sit here where there's a light — that is — " She glanced from one to the other, uncertainly. "I suppose I'm keeping you both up. Do you mind awfully?"

"A pleasure." He smiled, and lighted the cigarette, and sat down at a little distance on the bench beside the grand piano, and they were both more than ever aware that his mother would sit up as long as they did, silent and implacable and disapproving.

"I wish I could play that thing," she said desperately, making conversation. "I always wanted piano lessons when I was a little girl, but mother said none of our family was musical and it would be wasted on me. I suppose now I'll never know if I *could*."

He half turned towards the instrument and began idly to tick out a melody with one finger in the treble.

"What's that?" she asked, alert and listening, and the notes stopped.

"It's out of tune," he said.

"Can *you* play?" She rose and went to the piano. "Can you? Oh, please play something — just to make a noise!"

He laughed, and reached to lay his cigarette in an ashtray on the piano top, and she saw that there were several other butts already there, as though it were his habit. . . .

"Well, if you only want a noise — " he said indulgently, but his fingers were gentle and light on the keys, and he played from memory and with what even an untutored ear could recognize as a remarkably delicate touch the gay little intricate "Minute Waltz." And somehow it made no difference that the piano was not quite in tune.

"Oh, *Ridge!*" she cried, when it was so soon over. "*Oh*, what fun! Do it again!"

"The same one?" His face, lifted to hers as she leaned on the corner of the piano, was alight with tenderness as for a child.

"Are there more?" she cried.

"More Chopin? Dozens." He began again, one of the magic mazurkas, and the room was filled with the lisping rhythm of forgotten dancing feet.

"Oh, don't stop, don't *ever* stop!" she implored him. "It's what I've always wanted to do, to just sit down and play like that!"

"You can waste a lot of time at it," he said apologetically, his hands wandering on the keys. "At least, I do. It's an idle habit to get into."

"But you could play concerts, or — or on the radio — "

"Have you ever heard Iturbi?"

"Oh, yes, on records, but — "

"Then don't talk nonsense," he said briefly, and picked up the end of the cigarette and snuffed it out. His hand shook as he did so, and he rose almost angrily and swung away to the window and stood there staring out at the storm through the glass which ran with water as though it had been dipped in it, and the almost continuous lightning flares threw odd stripes of light and shadow across his white figure and cast his shadow high on the white wall behind him.

"Have I said something?" she asked faintly, standing where he had left her, and she thought, It was what *he* wanted to do, and she wouldn't let him.

But the storm was moving on at last, and a clock could be heard striking midnight. The rain still came down in sheets, and there was a little rivulet of water below the

[71]

sill, working across the wide, bare boards of the floor.

"This will settle the garden for this year," he said without resentment, stating a fact, changing the subject.

"Is the poor car still there?" She came to him at the window, but before he could reply there was a pounding on the front door, frenzied and distinct above the rolling thunder.

V I I

It was a strangely unnerving sound, at that time of night and in the midst of the storm, spelling dire emergency, but Ridge's movements were collected and swift as he caught up a flashlight from a table and started for the hall.

"Find out who it is before you open the door!" his mother called after him, but he took no notice, and the door swung back to reveal an old colored man propped against the outer casing gasping for breath. He was hatless and drenched, with water running out of his clothes and shining on his bald head in the beam of Ridge's flashlight.

"Marse Ridge — come quick — de Colonel hurt bad — "

"What happened?" Ridge pulled him inside and shut the door on the wind. The upturned flashlight in his hand illumined both their faces in the dim hallway — the wet black face of the old Negro, and Ridge's, white and tense — while the sinister lightning jumped and shimmered through the windows behind them.

"He get caught in de storm comin' home fum town — he try to keep comin', get home safe — I watchin' fo' him

— I know he comin', somewheh — den I see de lights ob de cah — I say T'ank-de-Lawd, I run out — " The man threw up both hands to his eyes in an operatic gesture of grief and horror. "I seen it — I *seen* de tree comin' down — I holler — I run — it ketch de cah right down de middle — two foot mo' an' I neveh git him out — but I done it, suh — I git him into de house, I tote him lak a baby in dese yeah arms — fah as de sofa in de parloh — he still dere, Marse Ridge — I don' dare move him up stairs to bed — he bleedin' awful — cain't stop de blood nohow — " The old Negro collapsed against the wall, rocking himself, his face hidden in his hands.

"All right, Jeb, I'll come with you." Ridge flung open the door of a coat closet and tore a mackintosh from a peg.

"Take my car!" Mary called quickly. "As far as you can, anyway!"

"It's one of those fancy new hydromatics," said Ridge. "I've never driven one, I'd smash it."

"Then I'll come — I'll drive it!" She snatched up her own coat from the chair where he had spread it to dry and ran into the hall.

"Would you?" he said, wondering.

"Of course. Let's get going."

"Wait a minute." He turned and ran up the stairs, sure-footed in the dim light, and returned at once with a bottle of whiskey which he thrust into the pocket of his rain-coat, and reached for the door.

His mother's voice floated after them.

"Ridge, that's your good suit — "

Guided by the lightning as much as by the flashlight in Ridge's hand, they ran toward the car. When they reached it, old Jeb halted and said, "I'm too soppin' wet to git in dere — "

"Hurry up, jump in!" Mary cried. "We can't go without you! Get in the back seat."

Obediently he climbed in through the door Ridge held open against the wind. She slid under the wheel and Ridge was beside her, slamming the door. There was some trouble with the starter, but at last it caught and she swung cautiously round the end of the tree, which did not quite block their way.

"To the right on the road," Ridge said quietly.

Shivering flares of lightning drowned the headlights every few seconds and the road ran with water. There were glimpses of wild, tossing trees and fountains of rain. The windshield-wiper strove faithfully, the wheel jumped and twisted in her hands.

"Take it easy," said Ridge. "Don't try to make time or we'll never get there."

"I don't remember seeing another house for miles. Does it show from this road?"

"No, it doesn't. There's a left turning about two miles along — it's around that bend. Where did the tree come down?" he asked over his shoulder of the back seat.

"Inside de gate — we gots to leave de cah dere — run fo' it 'cross de yahd — lady spoil heh shoes, suah — "

"Shoes don't matter," Mary said between her teeth. "Who is it, Ridge? Where are we going?"

"Old Colonel Ervine. Known him all my life. Taught me all I know about anything that matters — "

"Oh, Ridge, I'm sorry — "

"He's got nobody left now but Jeb. Lives here at Avalon all alone. I ought to have kept track of him better — I ought to do his errands for him — "

"You couldn't have foreseen anything like this."

"I could have driven his car into town for him today — Here you are, on the left. Look out, there's always a mud hole here — "

Groaning, the little car made the turn, water fanning out from the wheels, rocked violently, righted itself, and crawled on up a mere cart-track into the wilderness, towards the house called Avalon, where Ridge had gone for comfort and advice since boyhood. Stealing a frightened glance at his face in the light from the dashboard, Mary saw him sitting quietly, rigid with self-control, waiting for her to get him there, trusting her to get him there in the car he could not drive himself. Fortitude and pride. The stuff he was made of, inside. The only stuff that counted when the chips were down. The stuff you were born with, that you couldn't learn, and that you never could altogether lose. It held fast at Yorktown, and in the reeking, snake-infested swamps of the Santee, at Manassas, the Argonne, and the Bulge, and in the Pacific. She knew that Ridge was on the rack as they drove towards Avalon, it showed in the lines of his face, in his motionless hands, in his silence. But that was the only way it showed.

A light glimmered faintly through a distant window, and he said, "Gate-posts here — left again — whoa, there's the tree. Well, that's the end of his car, isn't it." The shabby little Ford was barely visible with the lower branches of the tree across it.

"Done broke his new bottle ob likker too," Jeb muttered as they stepped out into the storm again.

"Lucky I remembered mine." Ridge took Mary's arm. "Come on — run for it."

Splashing, slipping, jumping half-seen obstacles in the blob of light from his electric torch, they arrived on the porch, soaked to the knees, with rain running into their eyes and off their chins. The colored man pushed open the door and they entered a spacious hall, entirely bare of furniture except for one great mahogany cabinet against the wall opposite the sweep of the stairway leading up. The light was in a room on the right, and Jeb made for it, and they heard his voice as Ridge helped her out of her coat and took off his own, removing the whiskey bottle from the pocket. There was an ancient hat-rack fastened to the wall beside the door, and he hung them there, and puddles instantly began to form on the bare, polished floor beneath them.

"You'd better wait here till I see how it is," he said, but she followed him timidly to the doorway of the lighted room, feeling weak in the knees, wanting a chair.

In the dim glow cast by a kerosene lamp on the table, she saw an old man lying on a sofa with Jeb bending over him. Ridge's white suit picked up the light as he joined them, his quiet voice was clear and encouraging as he said, "Well, this is quite a night, isn't it! Can I be of any use?"

"Ridge? That you, Ridge — ? How did you get here?"

"Heard you'd had an accident, sir. Thought I'd come and see if you're all right."

"Don't think I am, Ridge — don't think I am — " It broke off on a grunting groan and there was silence.

Ridge straightened from the sofa and saw Mary coming towards him across the room and moved swiftly to meet her, blocking her view of the sofa with his body.

"This won't do for you. Go and sit down, I'll handle it."

"Can't I do anything to help?"

He hesitated.

"Do you know anything about first aid?"

"No. But I could do what you tell me. Is it bad?"

"Yes, it is. Can you stand the sight of blood without fainting?"

"I don't know. I can try."

"If you could help me with him I could send Jeb straight on after the doctor."

"Then let me try."

He pressed her shoulder briefly, with impersonal gratitude, and began to give his quiet orders.

"Jeb, bring me some more linen — a sheet to tear up and

a lot of towels. Then bring some water in a basin." He put the flashlight into Mary's hand. "The dining-room is across the hall. Go and find a tumbler or a cup — something he can drink out of."

The feeble spot of light preceded her, wavered across an oval mahogany table in the middle of the dining-room, died out before a livid blaze of lightning through uncurtained windows, and picked up a cabinet on the far wall. She opened the glass door and took a cup from a row of hooks — fragile, eggshell china — and carried it back to Ridge.

As she approached the sofa this time she got her first real look at what lay there, and recoiled instinctively from the bloodstained garments and cloths on the floor beside it, and the labored sounds of pain which came from the distorted face of the old man. Ridge's coat was off and his sleeves were rolled up. His hands, as he took the cup from her and poured whiskey into it, were already smeared with blood.

"Here you are, sir," he said easily, and raised the Colonel's head with an arm behind the pillow. "Nothing like a drink, you know — you'll feel better right away — "

Gasping, slobbering, obedient, the Colonel gulped it down and lay back, looking up into Ridge's face.

"Helps a lot," he said, and tried to smile. "Funny, how it helps — damn' tree — broke my new bottle — can't seem to — keep the stuff in the house any more — "

Jeb returned with a folded sheet and a pile of towels.

[79]

"Now the basin of water," said Ridge patiently, and added as the man turned away, "Leave a lamp burning in the kitchen." He picked up a towel and spoke to Mary, turning his back on her to bend over the sofa. "Tear the sheet into towel-sized pieces. Then make a couple of strips about three inches wide."

Jeb came back with the water.

"Bring another lamp," said Ridge, without looking up.

The lamp came, wavering a bit in Jeb's hand.

"Beside the other one," said Ridge. "Now go straight to the Dunhams at Live Oaks, and if their phone isn't working keep right on into town and find the doctor. Don't come back without him. Tell him I'm here."

"Yassuh. I do dat."

"Let him take your rain-coat, Ridge," said Mary, and they both paused to look at her in mutual surprise. "He's drenched," she said, patient with their preoccupation. "If there's no time for him to change his clothes, let him at least take your coat."

"Take my coat, Jeb," said Ridge, turning back to the sofa.

"Yassuh — thank you, ma'am," said Jeb, and was gone.

They were alone again, with the storm outside and the dreadful sounds on the sofa, mingled with the tearing of cloth in Mary's hands. As fast as she added to the pile of torn linen Ridge depleted it, so that she barely kept ahead with the supply. She realized that the storm had diminished at last, and the long windows were greying with dawn. The Colonel was quieter now, apparently comforted by whatever Ridge was doing for him.

"Can you come round here and hold this," Ridge said suddenly, and she nerved herself to whatever came next, to blood on her own hands — it was soon there. "Your hand is smaller than mine — slip it under him as flat as you can and pull this through," he said tersely.

Tight-lipped, she put her hands where he told her, caught hold of an end of the linen, held a sort of cloth plug over the crushed body while he bound it lightly in place — until at last the thing was decently done, and except for a slow seep of fresh blood around the edges, it seemed as though they had stopped the flow.

"That will have to do till the doctor comes," he said, with a sigh. "There's an inside kitchen beyond the dining-room, and Jeb left a light there. Go wash your hands. Then go upstairs to the Colonel's bedroom, the second door on the left, and find a blanket, or something to cover him with."

It was light enough now to see her way around the house without a flashlight. She found the kitchen and washed at the sink in cold water with laundry soap, went upstairs and found the blanket, and returned with it to Ridge in the parlor.

"Put it over him," he said, "and sit here till I come back. Don't leave him, will you."

He went away to the kitchen to wash, and when she had covered the still figure with the worn white blanket she sat down facing the sofa, her hands in her lap.

The Colonel lay quiet, his eyes closed, breathing in feeble gusts with pauses when she listened anxiously for the next intake. It always came, just when she dreaded that it never would. He had a fine, handsome head, with thick white hair, a beaky nose, and a long, humorous mouth. His face was deeply lined, and his body was spare to emaciation, as though perhaps he did not eat enough.

His eyes opened, and he lay looking at her without surprise, with a kind of pleasure.

"Alice?" he said faintly.

"I'm Mary. I came with Ridge."

"Any more — of that whiskey?"

"I think so. Ridge will be back in just a minute. He'll give it to you."

"Ridge — been in the Army — knows what to do," said the Colonel between his labored breaths. "Don't let him fool you — about all that — it wasn't Iwo Jima, but — held down very nasty spot — without much help — long time — before relieved. Won't own up — they gave him — some medal or other — have to get him drunk — to get the story — maybe not then — where's Ridge . . . ?"

"Coming, sir." The calm voice spoke almost gaily from the doorway. "How about another drink?"

"Just what I — had in mind," the Colonel said, and Ridge poured a liberal allowance into the cup and held it for him, sitting beside the sofa. "Have some — yourself," the Colonel suggested, between sips.

[82]

"Not just now, thanks. Later, maybe."

"Shouldn't ever — pass up a drink."

"Bit early in the day for me, sir."

"Jeb — get hurt too?"

"Oh, no — Jeb's gone for the doctor to fix you up."

"Feels better," gasped the Colonel. "Feels much better now. Did you learn — that in the Army?"

"Yes, that's one of the things they taught me in the Army."

"Thought I saw Alice — sitting here." The Colonel tried to lift his head to see around Ridge's shoulder.

"It's Mary, sir. She's staying with us."

"Don't mean to say — Let's have another look at her."

Mary stood up, smiling, where he could see her.

"Don't mean to say — you got yourself a girl — at last," said the Colonel.

"Well, not exactly. You see — "

"Yes, he has," said Mary, and laid an arm around Ridge's shoulders.

"Well, by damn," said the Colonel, and his face contorted between laughing and crying. "Never thought I'd — live to see the — day. She'll take — the nonsense out of you — pretty fast. Better'n you deserve — "

"Much better, sir."

"Where'd she come from — no place round here — "

"I'm a Yankee, sir," said Mary. "But I'm willing to learn."

"Well, by damn," said the Colonel. "He's the one's — got to learn."

[83]

"Let's finish your whiskey, sir," said Ridge, presenting the cup.

The Colonel drank it all and lay back, his eyes closed. Ridge reached under the blanket and drew out one of the Colonel's hands, holding it in both his, his finger unobtrusively on the pulse while he watched the ragged breathing.

Mary sat looking at them in the growing light as the new day washed out the kerosene lamps — thinking how tired Ridge looked, and how kind, and what a comfort it would be, if you were old and frightened, to have Ridge come and hold your hand.

"Ridge," said the Colonel again, without opening his eyes.

"I'm here, sir."

"Ridge, it's no use — I'm not going to last — "

"I wouldn't say that, sir. The doctor will be here soon."

"Want to say — what I've got left is yours, Ridge — since Alice went — not worth much now — but I wrote it down for you — years ago when Alice went — it's legal — "

"Now, hold on, sir, we're not going to give up yet!"

"Bring that girl — here to Avalon," said the Colonel. "It wants fixing up — but better than — two women under one roof. Like to have — you living here with — pretty wife — "

"Now, you wait a minute," Ridge said firmly. "We'll get you mended so you forget all about this."

"Yankee girl — good for you — shake you up a bit — she still here?"

"I'm here," said Mary steadily.

"You get him out of — that house — make him **stand up** to her — put up fight for him — you hear me?"

"I hear, sir."

"Don't take any back talk — from her — time somebody stood up to her — for once — Ridge won't — he's hell-bent always be a gentleman — to his mother — you Yankees — think you won the war — let's see how you do — when it's Fanny Creston — you're up against — got to fight for him — he's worth it, you know — "

"I know that, sir," said Mary.

"Ridge — "

"Don't try to talk any more now, sir."

"This Yankee girl — your last chance — you hear me, Ridge? — don't lose — your last chance — " And as Ridge was slow to answer, looking down at the thin veined hand in his, the Colonel shifted his head uneasily, his eyes came open. "Don't just sit there — lemme hear you say it — promise to hold out — this time — "

"I'll try, sir."

"Try — " Again the fretful movement of the Colonel's head. "Not good enough — promise — *promise* — " He attempted to struggle up, and Ridge laid gentle arms around him, easing him back to the pillow.

"Yes, yes, I promise — don't worry about it now, sir — just get well in time for the wedding — "

After a moment more the room was very still, because the ragged, painful breathing had stopped.

[85]

Ridge rose slowly, wearily, and stood looking down at the sofa. At last he turned away towards the windows, pink now with the rising sun, and stared blindly out at the devastated dooryard and the crumpled car.

Mary came to him, with a glance over her shoulder.

"Did he — die?" she whispered.

"Yes, he's gone. It wasn't any use."

"You knew all along he was going to die?"

"Oh, yes. But I had to pretend not."

"Oh, Ridge, you're wonderful!" She laid her cheek against his sleeve, holding his arm in both her hands.

"I'm sorry this had to happen to you," he said, not moving. "I wanted you to have — well, pleasant memories of this place."

"It happened to you too. And you loved him."

"All my life."

"Who was Alice?"

"His daughter. Dead fifteen years at least. He hadn't anybody else."

"He had you."

"I was a disappointment to him."

"But you made it easy for him, at the end."

"I tried to."

"He held to you. I watched you sitting there beside him, and I thought, 'Oh, Ridge, I love you so!' Maybe it's wrong to say that now, in this room — so soon. But it pleased him, to think that I loved you."

"That's the Dunhams' car," said Ridge, as a tidy convertible drew up beside theirs near the gate-posts. "They've brought Jeb back. Must have telephoned for the doctor."

"Poor Jeb," she said, as the three figures crossed the yard, instinctively avoiding the deepest puddles. "What becomes of him now?"

"I'll look after him somehow. He can stay on here — or at Fleetwood."

With the arrival of Ridge's friends to sustain him, and the awareness of all that must now be done for the Colonel in the ritual of burial, Mary was overtaken by a swift exhaustion, an overwhelming desire to lie down somewhere, anywhere, quite alone. She had had a punishing drive to reach the hotel, and then the emotional impact of the scene with Ridge at the Fountain. On top of that came the storm and the fantastic evening at Fleetwood, followed by the Colonel's death, the first she had ever witnessed. Almost twenty-four hours of continuous, interlocking tensions, all new to her, and any one of them tremendous in itself. The garden blurred unexpectedly while she looked at it, and she turned from the window, closing her eyes on the sharp morning light, while the floor seemed to tilt and lurch beneath her feet, so that she caught at the back of a chair and said quite steadily, but not daring to open her eyes — "I'll go back to the hotel now. You'll have things to do here — "

Ridge's arms closed round her from behind, quick and kind.

"My dear, forgive me — this has been terrible for you,

[87]

and I have just realized — you must rest, you must come and lie down, and Jeb will make some coffee — "

"I'm all right," she said obstinately, but faintly, holding to the chair. "I just — "

"Come along to Alice's room and lie down," said Ridge, and she heard the screen door open and close for the Dunhams' entrance into the house.

Mary set her teeth and raised her head and opened her eyes, and walked in the guiding circle of Ridge's arm towards the hall.

"Yes, he's gone," she heard Ridge saying as they reached the threshold. "There wasn't any hope, I saw that as soon as I came."

"Oh, poor Ridge, what a thing for you," said Mrs. Dunham softly. "The doctor will be right behind us, he was at home when we phoned."

"This is Mary Carmichael," said Ridge, as though no further explanation were needed. "She helped me to do what we could for him. It's time she had some rest now."

Mrs. Dunham had only to look at Mary and she took the politely extended little cold hand into both her motherly hands.

"You're feeling faint," she said. "And no wonder. You come along with me."

Ridge's supporting arm was exchanged for Mrs. Dunham's, and Mary was led into the tranquil room behind the parlor which had been Alice's sitting-room — the only one which had not been stripped of its possessions for the antique market. Alice's grand piano was there, her exquisite needlepoint covered the chairs, there were always fresh flowers in the vases. Blindly, with a boundless gratitude, Mary felt the sofa receive her unresisting body.

"There," said Mrs. Dunham gently. "You can be quiet here, in Alice's room. When did you eat last?"

"I don't remember," Mary confessed, trying not to mumble. "I'm — quite all right — "

And a beautiful blackness closed over her.

She roused to a cool wet cloth passing over her temples, and Mrs. Dunham's voice — "There we are — that's my girl — hold up, now, there we are — "

Mary sat up abruptly, and the room spun.

"How silly — I never fainted in my life — don't tell Ridge — "

"All right, we won't tell Ridge. But you lie down and stay right there till the doctor comes."

"I don't need the doctor, I'm quite all right now — " Mary sank back prudently against the pillow. "It was because of driving all day, and then the storm — please don't let Ridge know — "

"He won't know if you stay here quietly, the way he wants you to. If you try to get up now you'll likely fall flat on your face. There's the doctor coming in, I think — somebody with him, sounds like. You lie still, and I'll send Ridge along presently. We can look after things for him here; he'll have to go in town about the coffin, anyway."

When Mrs. Dunham had gone Mary lay listening to the

strange, muted sounds in the house — the sound, soon extinguished, of Jeb's honest grief — other sounds, slow and careful, which meant that the Colonel's body was being moved from the sofa up the stairs to his bedroom — sounds of new arrivals in the hall, subdued voices, more feet on the stairs. . . .

She opened her eyes and let them travel incuriously around the room which was Alice's. She wondered about Alice, lying there in her sanctuary. Dead all those years, and the room still hers, untouched, inviolate. Had she died young, or a devoted spinster daughter, living with her father? Perhaps if she had not died Alice would now be Ridge's age, and things would be different. No, unless Alice was the child of the Colonel's middle age, she would be older than Ridge. How much older? Would Alice have mattered to Ridge? There were pictures on the mantelpiece and on the round mahogany table — small framed pictures, placed there before Alice died fifteen years ago — perhaps pictures of Ridge as a boy — with Alice. . . .

Mary closed her eyes. It was past, it was not for her. But what was Alice going to think about the Colonel's expressed wish that Ridge should bring a Yankee bride to Avalon? The little framed pictures would be watching. Would they mind? . . .

The room itself seemed to answer her, with its tranquillity and shelter. The room had already accepted her into its safekeeping. Secure and comforted on Alice's sofa, Mary drifted into sleep.

V I I I

SHE WOKE WITH RIDGE'S HAND LAID CARE-
fully on hers — "Mary, we can go now, after you've had
something to eat." She woke without a start, slowly, con-
tentedly, and lay looking up at him, still drowsy and relaxed. There was the brisk, normal morning fragrance of
coffee in the air.

"I was asleep," she told him superfluously, a little surprised, but pleased.

"Fast asleep, I hated to wake you." Freshly shaved, and
with his brushed hair still damp, he himself obviously had
not slept. "You look very sweet, lying there. But Jeb has
fixed us some breakfast and they've put out clean towels
and things in a room upstairs. Mrs. Dunham said to send you
up there before you ate."

"But that's an awful bother, I can get some breakfast at
the hotel — " She sat up more cautiously this time, and spent
a moment trying to shake herself awake.

"Jeb would be very disappointed if you did that," he said,
and helped her to her feet.

[91]

She paused in her tracks, looking up at him.

"Ridge, are you all right?"

"Yes, I'm all right," he said, smiling down at her, and he touched the tip of her nose with the tip of his forefinger. "Go wash your face, that will bring you to."

So Mary climbed the stairs and passed the closed door of the Colonel's room on the left to enter the doorway where Mrs. Dunham was awaiting her.

"This is the room Ridge always has when he stays here," Mrs. Dunham said. "We've slicked it up for you, and Jeb has brought hot water for you to wash in. I think you'll find everything you need." She went away, moving noiselessly, pulling the door to behind her.

When Mary went downstairs again Ridge was in the hall, smoking a cigarette. They went into the dining-room and found four places laid along the sides of the table, in traditional hospitality, and Ridge pulled out a chair for her and sat down beside her.

Jeb came in with the coffee pot, and when she looked up at him to say Good-morning Mary saw with a pang that his cheeks shone with tears even while he went about his duties to his dead master's guests. He brought them fried eggs and hominy after the coffee, and Mary waited tactfully for the toast which never came.

Peeping through a crack in the kitchen door, Jeb observed that she wasn't eating much, and cast a desperate glance around the kitchen for something else to offer her. Peaches? He had brought in some nice peaches the day before for the Colonel's supper. He put some on a plate and carried them doubtfully into the dining-room.

"Lady lak a peach so early in de mawnin'?" he ventured, setting them down in front of her.

"Oh, thank you, Jeb, I could eat a peach," said Mary gratefully, and reached out for one, smiling up into his anxious face.

The old colored man blinked, gave her a tremulous grin, glanced at Ridge as though to say Don't let us lose this treasure, and departed to his kitchen with a full heart. She was brave with a car, she had sat the night out with his old master, she was dear to the man he felt sure would be his next master, she had a foolish fondness for peaches at breakfast, and she had given him his name with a smile. She belonged.

It was of course impossible for them to talk anything but commonplaces, with Jeb in the kitchen and the house full of coming and going. Two or three new arrivals, including the rector, came to the dining-room door and spoke quietly to Ridge, refused the proffered cup of coffee with thanks, and quietly went away, concealing, on such an occasion, their natural curiosity at Mary's presence. Whoever she was, and wherever she had come from, she had passed through the night's ordeal with Ridge, and was now one of them.

When Mary had eaten her peach, Ridge said with a kind of pity, "Would you like to go now?" and she rose quickly in assent.

"You needn't come with me, Ridge, if it's not convenient — "

"But it is. I have to go to town anyway — to the undertaker's."

"Oh," she said, remembering.

Wondering at his self-contained, unemotional acceptance of the sad duties of the next of kin, she went out into the hall with him, and saw that the parlor was being tidied and rearranged by neighbor women who had appeared from somewhere and quietly taken possession. The house smelled of fresh flowers and newly raised dust in a strange combination.

The doctor came out of the parlor and shook hands with Mary, looking down at her keenly in the merciless reflected sunlight from the porch. Ridge explained that he was going into town with her, and why, and the doctor nodded.

"When you've done that, go home and get some rest yourself," he said. "I'll stay here for a while. Your car still laid up?"

"I'll drive him home," said Mary, and when Ridge remarked that he'd catch a lift back from town somehow, she turned on him with authority. "You haven't had any rest at all and I have," she said. "I'll wait and drive you home, and no nonsense."

The doctor nodded again.

"That's the way to handle him," he said. "You take him home, and I'll send for him again this afternoon — about three."

"Thank you," Ridge said meekly, and they went out to her car.

It was going to be another hot day. The sun was already blazing, and the saturated ground steamed. For a while Ridge rode in silence, smoking, and she told herself that she must be careful of him, after so much shock and grief and no rest. But the question of what difference the shared experience of the past night and the promise exacted from him by the Colonel would make in their future could not be put down in her mind.

At last he turned towards her with his rueful smile.

"Well," he said wearily, "now you know the worst, don't you. Are you convinced?"

"Of what?" she asked blankly.

"That it won't do. That there's nothing for you at Fleetwood but disappointment and — humiliation. I have no sort of life to offer you."

"But, Ridge — " She was incredulous. "You *promised* him!"

"I would have said anything then — to help him."

"And you think he won't know if you go back on it?"

"That's a question, isn't it." He touched the end of his cigarette carefully to the ashtray on the dashboard, removing the ash. "I don't know the answer, do you?"

"I wouldn't like to risk it."

"And suppose he could know — somehow — that I was lying to him last night. At the same time wouldn't he be able to understand why?"

[95]

"You don't lie to a dying man, Ridge. That's one of the rules."

"I know." He sat motionless, drooping, his eyes fixed on the dashboard, and the cigarette trembled in his hand. "I don't lie to you either, if I can help it. It was all true — back there at the Fountain, before the rest of it happened. I want to keep you with me for the rest of my life more than I want salvation. After last night when you were such a soldier and didn't faint or squawk, I'm more in love with you than ever, if that's possible. You said something there by the window that I'll never forget — " He broke off, closed his lips firmly, as though he had said too much.

"What was that? What did I say?"

"You said — 'Ridge, you're wonderful!' " He gave an apologetic breath of laughter, which shook his slack shoulders. "Nobody around here ever said that to me before," he said.

"But you were! You knew just what to do and how to talk to him. You kept it decent and dignified — "

"No. He did that."

"Do you remember what he said about the house — because Alice was gone?"

"Yes, I remember."

There was a long silence in the car, which he would not break.

"Is it too soon to talk about it?" she ventured. "Isn't that the answer for us, Ridge? C-couldn't we live there, as he said — at least to start?"

"Live on what?" he asked evenly.

"Well, I don't know — perhaps — however you live now."

"There is a small annuity now, from insurance, paid quarterly to my mother. It never quite lasts out for two. So we sell things. That's why the house looks the way it does. The Colonel had a pension, and did the same. There is even less left at Avalon to sell. And it's in worse repair than Fleetwood."

She told herself that he was worn out and battered by the night's emotions, and it was wrong to press him further now. But she said doggedly —

"It would be a roof over our heads."

"It would," he agreed quietly. "But people have to eat too."

"Ridge, you promised not to give up again!" she cried desperately.

"Easy to say, at a time like that."

There was another long silence, while she drove. She was thinking of her own little money, invested so that she had about three hundred dollars a year, separate from her mother's income from her father's estate. He had wanted her to have her own spending-money after she was twenty-one. She was wondering what effect it would have on Ridge to mention that now, and willing as she was to use it in any possible way to establish their future she dared not suggest to him at this point that she was better off than he was.

"We can't talk like this in the car," she said miserably. "Where can we go, later on, to be private for a little while?"

"I suppose you think if I have a chance to kiss you again I will agree to anything," he murmured, lighting another cigarette from the end of the one he held, which he stubbed out in the ashtray with shaking fingers, and she flashed him a look of astonishment mixed with anger.

"What a thing to say!" she gasped. "How would you like it if I just let you out of the car in town and went straight back home and stayed there?"

"It would be the sensible thing for you to do."

"I haven't been sensible about you from the start, and I'm not going to start now."

"Try," he said. "It's not too late."

The car was entering the single main street of the little town.

"It's just here on the right," he said. "Back of the furniture store."

She stopped beside the curb, and he got out.

"You go back to the hotel and get some sleep," he advised her through the window. "Then see how you feel."

"I'll wait and drive you home first."

"I'm not in a very good position to refuse that," he said wryly. "Thank you. I won't be long here."

She sat with her hands on the wheel, numb and patient. It would all have to wait now, till he could think straight again. Should she offer to go to the funeral? She was after all an outsider. At least she could send flowers. There was no place to buy flowers in the town, that she knew of, but she would ask the woman behind the desk at the hotel.

After the funeral, Ridge would be more himself, they could decide things more sanely. But there was so little time, she had to send the telegram to Merriwether before the week was out.

Ridge didn't know about the waiting contract, and if he did, he would advise her to sign it. She recognized unwillingly now that she would have to sign it, if only out of decency to the college for expecting her to come to her senses and not leave them stranded. She was trapped at Merriwether until June. But if Ridge made good use of the time between now and June — what kind of use? — if he would only *try*. . . .

Put up a fight for him, the Colonel had said. Let's see how you do when it's Fanny Creston you're up against. Make him stand up to her, the Colonel had said. To do this, Mary knew that she would have to see Ridge again after she left him at Fleetwood this morning. It was awkward to insist upon that, it made her feel — pushing and possessive, detestable things in a woman. It was not right to force a man's hand. But the Colonel had pointed the way, with the legacy of Avalon. Ridge must be made to see that Avalon could save them, that Avalon was sanctuary, and must not be wasted. . . .

He came out and got into the car, looking drawn and exhausted. He must be allowed to rest, first of all. She turned back along the road by which they had come, and neither had spoken when they reached the turning which led to Avalon. Mary knew a moment of despair as they passed it

— Will I come back to it? she queried destiny. Will my life be there? . . .

She felt his eyes upon her face, and glanced at him. He was sitting sidewise, smoking, and watching her in his rueful way.

"Little saint," he said, as their eyes met, and hers went back to the road. "Why don't you just knock me over the head and leave me in the ditch?"

"It must be love," said Mary, with her inextinguishable gaiety, which came of cherishing, and comfort, and a happy childhood.

"I can't answer that," he said after a long moment, not quite sure of his voice.

When they reached Fleetwood, with its fallen tree still across the drive, he said, "Your picnic kit is still inside. I'll get it."

"I'll leave it here for now, I want to come back. We've got to talk."

"We can't talk *here!*" he said, surprised.

"I know that. But where, Ridge? At the Fountain we'd forget to."

He thought a minute, harassed, preoccupied, driven by a dozen considerations which were unknown to her.

"The doctor is sending a car at three to take me back to Avalon. I'll take the picnic kit along with me. If you don't come to Avalon by four o'clock, I'll bring it to the hotel and leave it at the desk."

"Is that to save my face if I want to run out on you now?"

"You could put it that way." He got out of the car and closed the door.

"I'll be at Avalon at four o'clock," she said, and drove away, and the tilt of her chin above the wheel straightened his back as he went up the steps to the house.

I X

S<small>HE REALLY WOULD RISK IT WITH ME, HE</small>
thought incredulously. Even after last night here, she is
ready to try it. I must measure up. I mustn't give in again.

Fleetwood had that watchful emptiness which means that
a place is occupied by someone who chooses to remain in-
visible. The picnic kit, its bottles re-capped, the remaining
food re-packed in the tin box, was set ready on the table in
the hall.

He went into the parlor and stood looking down at the
piano as though it might have some discernible message for
him since last night — the ashtray had not been emptied.
He wondered if he would ever play the "Minute Waltz"
again. Not if he lost her. Never if he lost her now.

There was a movement in the hall and he turned to see
his mother coming down the stairs. She walked stiffly, he
thought, and held to the bannister like an old woman. She
was old, he thought compassionately, and nobody cared a
pin for her, she had driven all affection from her and existed angrily in the ruins of her life. The Colonel was old
too, but tears would be shed for him by other people besides

black Jeb. He had friends. He had charm, and in his way he was enjoying himself still, right up to last night. There would be no one to mourn this sullen, resentful woman to whom Ridge owed at least filial allegiance. Her death would never be even to him the bereavement that the Colonel's loss had been.

"Well?" she asked impatiently, as he did not speak. "What happened? What became of you?"

"The Colonel died. His ribs were crushed into the wheel when the tree fell on the car."

"Were you there?"

"When he died? Yes."

"Did that girl spend the night with you?"

His lips tightened, but he let it pass.

"She waited with me until Jeb got to the Dunhams and they called the doctor and came to Avalon. Then she drove me into town to arrange about the coffin."

"What about that?" She pointed to Mary's picnic kit.

"I'm to take it to the hotel later."

"She won't be back here, then."

"That depends," he said, and took a deep breath. "That depends on me."

It surprised her. She gave him a quick glance, and passed him into the room and sat down in her usual chair with her crochet work. He got out a cigarette and lit it. His hands were shaking and he felt sick.

"I want to marry her," he said.

"Is she willing?"

"Oddly enough, yes."

"What's her game?"

He felt the helpless, futile rage rising within him, and bore down on it resolutely.

"She hasn't any game. We seem to understand each other. We've been writing for several months, and we've fallen in love."

"Doesn't she understand that there's nothing in it for her?"

"Except me. She seems to attach some importance to me. Funny, isn't it."

He waited. She went on crocheting impassively, remote, divorcing herself from this wholly fantastic new idea of his.

"Do you want to bring her here to live?" she inquired at last with hostility.

"No. I don't."

"Then I'm not thrown out."

"Of course not. Fleetwood is yours." He could not bring himself to tell her about the Colonel's legacy, and he had no right, anyway, till the will was read.

"Then what has it got to do with me?" she was saying.

"Nothing, I suppose."

"Except that if you leave here with her you'll have nothing to live on. Unless you can earn something, which you never have yet. Or can she support you, as I have done?"

He made the most futile and inconclusive of all replies. With a look of hatred he turned and left the room.

Upstairs in his bedroom he locked the door, got into pajamas, and lay down on the bed. The hot, waterlogged air hardly stirred at the open windows.

He thought about Mary at the hotel, wondered if she were asleep by now. He knew the Colonel's house as well as his own, and he tried to picture her there, moving about the familiar rooms — living there with him, as his wife — always there, if he put out a hand to touch her, as she had been this morning, on Alice's sofa — just the two of them, alone together, complete and apart from the world, learning each other, building a life . . .

With what? It took money to live like that.

One of the houses might be sold, to put the other in repair. But neither would bring in much in their present condition. And that would mean two women under one roof. The Colonel was right, that wouldn't do.

If it hadn't been for the war he might have had some kind of law practice by now, some kind of living. It had been his own idea, going into law, for even in his father's time, when there had been capital to lose each year, the place had not paid for itself in the way it had once done. During his own minority his mother's methods had completed its ruin. He had never meant to try to get a living out of Fleetwood, even before the dam went in. There was still some timber to cut, and more should be set out at once. There was still some game, which would at least help to provide food for the house. Properly handled, Fleetwood might again pay its taxes and upkeep. But what money there

[105]

was left he could not touch, and his mother had no interest in making use of the resources that remained, so his hands were tied. And there wasn't much incentive, in daily association with a woman who in his absence had crossed the borderline into madness, driving away from her all companionship, alienating the patience even of her kin. He did not know what to do about her, he felt that she should not be left entirely alone as she was constantly daring him to do, and so he stayed there in his odd, weary way, and time passed.

In his lonely, self-sufficient boyhood he had chosen law as a profession which would finally set him free of her, even free of Fleetwood, and with which he intended to support himself. He had passed his exam without difficulty, and had been admitted to the Bar, but before the ink was dry on his papers the war had claimed him, and the Pacific. He came home after three years away, without prospects, his health deteriorated, weary in spirit, wanting only to rest and be quiet, and find himself in peace.

Always solitary and self-contained, he became steadily more so, erecting a barrier of studied indifference between himself and the world which before long nobody but the Colonel could penetrate — because for the Colonel it simply wasn't there. Some men, younger men, had gone back to school and learned a trade, or refreshed an old profession, on the G.I. Bill of Rights. But he couldn't suddenly now begin at the bottom to establish a law practice. Or could he? Did he remember any of it? He tried, and his mind went blank.

Well, there you were. Ten years. It was gone. Not much in it anyway, nowadays. What had become of those ten years?

He had been over it so many times, and there was never any answer. He turned his face into the pillow in a familiar gesture of despair. Was Mary lying like this at the hotel, sleepless, waiting to be together again? It was still a long time till four o'clock. Would she come? She had said she would. She had more guts, anyway, than he had now. She faced things.

And what would happen then? They would kiss, hopelessly, in the quiet room above the garden which would have been her sitting-room as it was Alice's — the Colonel had kept that unchanged, no matter what happened to the rest of the house. But if he kissed her the world would fall apart again into shimmering, nonsensical glory where one didn't think at all. He mustn't come to that now.

The General. What did he do when he was at the end of his rope. He came out swinging, Mary said. He lost the battle, but he won the war. Ridge sat up, and locked his arms around his knees. Something there. You lost the battles, but you won the war. It was the same in the Pacific. You kept on taking it, but you never quite got knocked out. Could he go through that sort of thing again? Could he do it just once more, even for Mary? This time it would be worse than the Japs. This was the old battlefield and the old enemy, with a long record on his side of failure and despair.

He laid his forehead on his knees and shivered in the soggy heat.

[107]

X

THE CAR WHICH CAME FOR HIM A LITTLE before three was driven by the doctor himself — the same man who had seen Ridge's father die, and a few days later had brought Ridge into the world. He perceived, as the slack figure in white came down the steps towards him, that demoralization was setting in.

"I came myself," he said, when Ridge was in the car, "because I want to talk to you."

Ridge made no reply.

"It's bound to hit you hard," the doctor said, busy with his driving. "I know what the old man meant to you. You don't want me to go on about it, do you, but I'm going to, all the same."

Ridge made no reply.

"Did you know that he had left you Avalon in his will?" asked the doctor.

"Yes. He told me last night."

"I witnessed the will some years ago. *'Everything of which I die possessed,'* it says."

"Except his courage," Ridge said, and the doctor glanced at him quickly, and away.

"He wouldn't think you needed that. What I wanted to say was this. He took thought for you. If he'd had a million, he'd have left it all to you. But he gave you what he had — solitude — privacy. Go and live in that house, Ridge, alone, and save your soul."

"I know," said Ridge, and passed a hand across his face. "I know exactly what you mean."

"If you don't go," said the doctor, his eyes on the road, "you're the one that will be taken away in a straitjacket, not your mother."

"I know. Have you ever thought *why* she would like to see me dead? I've always let her alone."

"It's simple enough, Ridge, in a complicated sort of way. You look exactly like your father. But you're the son. And you're alive. Almost."

"Oh, Lord," said Ridge, beginning to realize.

"The line between love and hate is very fine," the doctor went on. "Especially in an unbalanced mind. Your mother's jealousy was psychopathic for some time before your father's death. I don't suppose you ever knew that she once threatened his life with one of his own guns."

"I'm not exactly surprised," Ridge said, after a moment. "What happened?"

"He was man enough to take the gun away from her," the doctor said rather grimly. "He came and told me about it because he was even then concerned about the very thing that eventually happened — that a child of his might be left in her care. Has it been pretty bad?"

"It hasn't been good," said Ridge, with his wry smile. "It occurs to me that I haven't much of a heritage for any possible children of my own."

"You're all Creston," said the doctor. "I'd be willing to risk that."

"He must have had a screw loose himself, to marry such a woman."

"You may find it hard to believe, but at the time of their marriage she seemed to be simply a handsome, high-spirited girl," said the doctor.

"I suppose there was no doubt about how he was killed," Ridge suggested thoughtfully.

"Fortunately not. He was riding one of those horses of his that nobody else could manage. Probably the mastery of a rebellious animal was some relief to his feelings. But it was not his habit to be thrown by them. He died without regaining consciousness."

"Was she glad?"

"Glad he died?" The doctor stole another glance at him. "She was apparently beside herself with grief which had a kind of rage in it. She was right in a way to have the horse destroyed, it was a brute. But I was with her constantly on account of you — I wasn't at all sure of saving you in the circumstances — and it was quite plain that you represented an intrusion rather than a solace. I suppose nowadays it would be considered a case for a psychiatrist," he added ruefully. "At that time, everyone merely hoped that time would do its usual work and she would find comfort in his child. Did she ever?"

"Never."

The doctor sighed.

"There was no one with the authority to take you away from her. The Colonel tried, you know."

"I didn't know," said Ridge, motionless.

"Oh, yes, he tried. Byron Conway could tell you all about it, he drew up the Colonel's will some years ago — he'll be there today to talk to you about that. You have no co-heirs, and there will be no search for witnesses — so there will be no delay. I advise you to go and live at Avalon as soon as possible."

"There's just one thing," said Ridge. "Once in a while I have to eat. You don't seem to realize the fantastic fact that I haven't even got pocket money of my own."

"Then we must find a way to get you some," said the doctor.

"That's fine," said Ridge, without enthusiasm. "There are so many jobs around here that I'm qualified for."

"Must be something you can do."

"Anything I can think of a Negro can do better."

The doctor thought hard, and came up with an idea.

"You can play the piano," he said.

"I play the wrong kind of music."

"He always kept Alice's piano tuned."

"Yes. It's in better shape now than mine."

"You might give music lessons."

"Scales?" said Ridge, his amusement tinged with affection. "And what about the pupils? Do you bring them out in busloads, or what?"

"Ridge, if you don't mind my asking — where did that girl come from, this morning?"

"Massachusetts," said Ridge unhelpfully.

"Care to tell me about it?"

"Damn, I forgot her picnic kit. It's still at Fleetwood, and I promised to return it this afternoon."

"What have you done to deserve a girl like that?" demanded the doctor. "And where did you find her?"

So Ridge, who had never spoken of Mary to anyone but Mr. Morgan at the Museum before, partly out of a superstition that she would vanish if he did, like something in a fairy tale, told the doctor about the thesis, and the letters, and then found himself coming up against the necessity of explaining why she had come back. And just as he was about to balk at that, they reached the gates of Avalon and Mr. Conway was already there, and the subject of Mary was mercifully dropped.

Promptly at four o'clock her little car pulled up beside all the other cars which had gathered at Avalon that day. She had been given the freedom of a garden in the town to choose her own flowers for the Colonel, and had gathered a simple sheaf of gladiolas in gay light colors. Carrying these, feeling a little shy, a stranger at this time of close neighborhood solidarity, she walked slowly towards the steps.

It was the first time she had really looked at the house, which was bigger than Fleetwood, and at one time must have been grander. Now it was grey with lack of paint, but the garden was better kept than at Fleetwood — Jeb, no doubt — and the porticoed façade gazed back at her with enigmatic dignity. Almost, they eyed each other. You're beautiful, she told it respectfully. Please let me stay. I'll try very hard.

She mounted the steps and approached the screen door. There were voices within, low-pitched, but audible, and a muffled activity. The undertaker's chairs had arrived and were stacked in the hall, ready to be carried into the parlor which had been cleared to receive them. Flowers had arrived, and were banked temporarily around the foot of the staircase, awaiting their removal to the parlor after the coffin came down.

A thin, elderly man with tired, smiling eyes was stationed at the door and opened it to her without question. She hesitated on the threshold.

"Ridge — is expecting me," she said faintly.

"He's in Alice's room," said the doorkeeper. "Go right along in."

She crossed the hall, carrying her flowers, wondering if she had the right to lay them with the rest, and paused at the door of the sitting-room. She had time to see that Ridge was seated at the table with two other men before he rose

[113]

quickly and came to meet her. His face was gentle and alight for her, because he had tried not to expect her and yet in spite of himself had believed that she would come. His eyes went from her face to the flowers in her arms, and back again with unspoken gratitude.

"Mrs. Jennings at the hotel let me choose them myself from her sister's garden," she explained. "Are they all right like this? I've tied them."

"They're perfect. We'll put them down here, for now."

He took the gladiolas from her and laid them with the other flowers near the stairs.

"Am I too soon?" she asked timidly. "Shall I wait in the car?"

"By no means. Come in here with me." He laid an arm lightly around her waist and led her into Alice's room, where the doctor and Mr. Conway rose to greet her. "This," said Ridge, not for the first time, and with the same sensation of warm pride, "is Mary Carmichael."

They had got the story out of him by now, and their kind old eyes appraised her youth, her cotton-frocked simplicity, her disarming shyness. It was plain that they liked what they saw.

"I begin to understand," said the lawyer, who had been born a skeptic.

"They were both inclined to think you were after my money," Ridge explained to her in his rueful way, and Mary laughed round at them good-naturedly.

[114]

"Did you tell them I came all the way back here to get it?" she asked.

"I hadn't got as far as that."

"Just how far does it go?" asked the doctor.

"I'm trying to marry him, sir," said Mary, with a shining face.

"Any luck?" inquired the doctor, beetle-browed.

"He keeps bringing up the silly question of bread and butter."

"I'm surprised," said Mr. Conway. "As a matter of fact, we were just going into that." He took a turn around the table thoughtfully. "Ridge is at a crossroads," he said. "When you get to be my age, you have noticed that they come every so often even in what looks like a dead end. The Colonel has made Ridge a crossroads. That you should be here at the same time seems to me all a part of the pattern, whatever it may be." He paused and examined her sharply for signs of comprehension.

Mary nodded intelligently.

"I've noticed that, studying history," she said. "It makes a sort of design — a graph — in a man's life."

The two older men exchanged a glance as though they reached some agreement, and Mr. Conway went on.

"We have already dug it out of Ridge that you two are in love." He paused again for confirmation.

"Yes, sir," said Mary, and she smiled confidingly at him.

"You're rather a long way from home, aren't you?"

"It's all on account of the General, sir. I think he intended it," she explained.

"Possibly." The legal mind was indulgent. "Some years ago I made Ridge an offer. He didn't say Yes, he didn't say No, it just lay there. Today I have renewed it, in another form."

"Oh, not — " Mary took a step forward. "You don't mean — a *job!*"

"It was a job in the beginning," said the lawyer. "Now it has certain strings attached to it. And it pays less than it did."

"But it's work he can do," she insisted.

"That remains to be seen."

She turned, questioningly.

"Ridge . . . ?"

Ridge looked away, and went to stand at the window, his back to the room. In the silence, Mr. Conway began putting papers back into his brief-case, and the doctor picked up his hat.

"That's all for now," he said. "You and Mary will have things to talk over."

They went away together, leaving the silence in the room. Mary went to him, and touched his sleeve.

"What are the strings?" she asked timidly. "What sort of job is it?"

"Desk work," said Ridge. "Office-boy work. But primarily I must be industrious, ambitious, and sober over a period of time."

"Well, what's wrong with that?" she asked quietly. "I'll help. Ridge, I — got myself in kind of a jam about teaching next year, I — left it too long about coming back here, and — now they want me to sign a contract — "

"You are going back to Massachusetts today," he said evenly. "Contract or no contract."

"Oh, *Ridge* . . . !" She buried her face against his sleeve.

"It's not going to be any honeymoon here for a while," he said, not looking at her. "In the first place, I'm not sure I can do it, in the circumstances. They have made conditions which are — practically impossible."

"Such as — ?"

"Well, for one thing — I have to leave Fleetwood. I have to live here alone."

"But that's what the Colonel wanted, only he expected me to be here too. I should think you'd be glad — "

"I can't afford to hire an attendant for my mother," he went on, as though she had not spoken. "Besides, no one will stay in the house with her now."

"Well, then — "

"Well, I can't just leave her there!" he said impatiently. "I can't just walk out. Put yourself in my place. She's an old woman. She may be a hateful old woman, but it's not human to leave her utterly alone."

"But if even the *doctor* thinks — "

"Doctors come to look at things differently. They get very callous."

"Doctors get used to making hard choices, I think," she

said reasonably. "They try to save what's most worth while, don't they? After all, it isn't as though you would be a hundred miles away. You could have a telephone put in." She laid her hand on his sleeve again. "We might hire someone just to go and sleep in the house at night."

He moved aside, away from her hand.

"I shall have to live on borrowed money for heaven knows how long."

"That first day I came to Fleetwood, you said she was away on a visit. Couldn't she go back there for a while — wherever it was?"

He gave her one of his level, unwavering looks.

"She wasn't away," he said. "I simply felt it was impossible to ask you to come inside the house."

"Ridge — maybe now is the time to mention it. I have about three hundred a year of my own. I can't use the capital, but — living at home the way I do, it sort of accumulates in the bank — "

"You know perfectly well I wouldn't touch your money," he said, and because he was feeling flayed and raw, he said it ungently.

"But, darling, we — "

"*No*," he said abruptly. "This is my problem. Please leave me alone with it."

She had no experience with a man's exacerbated pride, and she stared at him, hurt and confused.

"Very well," she said, a little on her dignity. "I — guess I'd better go now." But at the door she turned, looking back at him. "The others seem to have gone. Can't I drive you home?"

He was about to refuse, and then he came towards her down the room.

"I forgot to bring the picnic kit. If you'll drive round that way I'll put it in the car."

"It doesn't matter," she said, not caring much about anything if she and Ridge were going to be strangers like this.

"Of course it matters. I saw it in the hall, but it slipped my mind again when the doctor came for me."

There was silence in the car most of the way. Mary was wondering if she must leave it like this, and go back to a dismal year of teaching at Merriwether, with only the hope that their letters could work the same magic again. Ridge, enmeshed in realities and decisions again, after so long a time in the anaesthetized half-world he had chosen to live in, was feeling sick and bewildered, and resentful against he knew not what. Worst of all he had taken it out on Mary, and now there was no time to undo that with tenderness and promises. There were no promises to make, as things stood with him now.

"I'm terribly sorry," he said hopelessly. "Will you forgive me?"

"I know it's hard on you, Ridge."

"That's not the point. I spoke to you as though you weren't Mary. I never meant to do that. You can see how it is — you'd never be able to put up with me."

"Just because you were cross?" she said bravely. "I'd be a fine wife if I couldn't stand a little of that."

"Mary — my darling — I can't marry you until I have done something about my life. I have to start it all over again. It may take quite a while. I'm not even going to ask you to wait. It might be all for nothing."

"If I could only stay here to see it through with you —"

"No. When I have done it — if I can do it — we'll talk about that."

"How long will it take?"

"I don't know. In the meantime you must go back to Massachusetts. And when you get there look around you — and if you see anything better, take it and be happy!"

"When may I come back here?"

"Not till I send for you."

"But we can't say Good-bye like this!"

"It looks as though we've got to," he said, for the car had reached his gates.

With the empty, watching windows of the house before them there was no chance to linger, no time for anything more to be said between them. She turned into the drive and brought the car to a stop.

Something lay on the gravel at the bottom of the steps, as though it had been thrown there from the porch. They recognized it without words. It was the picnic kit which he had forgotten in the hall.

He got out of the car and picked it up, and it tinkled with the shattered glass of the insulated bottles. His face was white. He opened the car door and set the wrecked kit on the back seat.

"Don't worry about this any more," he said, very low. "I'm leaving here tonight."

"Oh, thank God, Ridge, I'm *afraid* for you to stay here!"

"There's nothing to be afraid of," he said, in that voice which was, even for him, unnaturally quiet. He looked at her, unsmiling, rigid, with a glitter of anger in his eyes. "I've had enough, now. I'm all through."

"Then I'm glad it happened. You'll go back to Avalon tonight?"

"As soon as I can get a few things into a bag."

"And you'll write often and — tell me how things are?"

"Yes. I'll write. Now and then. I shall be pretty busy, you know. Now, you get along out of here, fast." He reached in through the open window and laid his hand briefly on hers on the wheel. "Dear Mary," he said, and turned away towards the house, and without looking back heard the car reach the gates and take the road.

The lower floor was empty and vigilant. He went quickly up the stairs and into his room, jerked a suitcase from a shelf in the clothes closet to the bed, and began to fill it with the contents of the bureau drawers. He had only a few belongings worth packing. He added several books from the bedside table, and went into the bathroom across the hall for his shaving things and toothbrush.

On his way back to his room he came face to face with his mother near the door.

"What are you doing?" she asked sharply, as though he were a child of ten.

"I'm leaving," he replied, and passed her into the room, laid the things in the suitcase and closed the lid.

"Eloping?" she suggested from the doorway, her lips curled.

"In broad daylight, through the front door?"

"It's that girl," she said.

"Miss Carmichael is on her way home."

"Threw you over, did she!"

He picked up the suitcase and found that he could not pass her at the door.

"Colonel Ervine left Avalon to me in his will. I am going to live there, alone, and in peace."

"Before the funeral?"

"It won't be the first time I've taken refuge there."

"And what will you live on?"

"That's none of your business," he said, and tried again to pass her, but she stood squarely at the threshold, blocking the way.

She was nearly as tall as he was and weighed more. He felt the sweat running down his back and under his ribs. There was a singing in his ears. If he stepped back quickly he could close the door in her face, and lock himself in. . . .

"I forbid you to go," she was saying.

"I'm thirty-four. You can't forbid me to do anything. Please stand out of the way."

"Lay hands on me. I dare you to."

He put one arm across her chest to force her aside. Unexpectedly her body gave before him and as he moved forward he received a powerful push between the shoulder-blades, which, weighted and off-balance as he was with the suitcase, sent him hurtling towards the stairs. He caught at the banister, missed the top step, and fell heavily with the suitcase down the first flight to the landing.

Stupefied with surprise and the jar of his fall, he gathered himself slowly and saw her looking down at him over the railing at the top, waiting to see if he could get up. There was no remorse or anxiety in her face — only a sort of cold curiosity. He thought of his father, who had been man enough to take the gun out of her hands.

With an effort, he got to his feet, picked up the suitcase, and went down the lower flight and through the door, favoring a wrenched knee. Hampered by the suitcase, he crossed the drive and gained the road and hurried along it, while his breath came sobbingly. When the house was left behind he leaned against a tree beside the road and recovered himself slowly. It brought back to him other times when he had fled from his home, when he was much younger — only then he ran.

He went on slowly, limping, carrying the suitcase. To keep him from leaving the house and becoming his own man she had been ready to maim him — a broken leg was doubtless what she had hoped for. He could not but wonder if a broken neck would have suited her even better. She was mad, quite mad, and she might have got hold of Mary. Such a fall could have killed Mary, she had such tiny bones, like a bird's. He had done right to send Mary away, but how was he to live now that he had held her in his arms, so willing and so ignorant, and so blind? If she had known anything at all about men it would never have happened, she would have passed him by without a glance. And yet — the General intended it to happen, she said. The General had brought her here, had given them the magic hours at the Fountain — his legacy to them, as Avalon was the Colonel's. Sometimes there did seem to be a pattern. . . .

But there was no blueprint now, for the rest of the way. That was up to him. This was where he was supposed to come out swinging.

His knee was painful, and his head swam a bit, in the sun. He kept on walking, doggedly, till he came to the Colonel's gates, with the tree lying across the way. Most of the cars had gone now, till the funeral would bring them back.

Jeb saw him coming and met him at the top of the steps and took the suitcase from his hand.

"You come and set down quiet in Miss Alice's room," said Jeb, needing to ask no questions. "I fin' you a drink right away."

"Later," said Ridge, and paused in the hall, breathing unevenly. The flowers were still there around the staircase, though the undertaker's chairs were now in place in the parlor.

"Coffin don' come till de mawnin'," said Jeb quietly. "De Colonel an extra tall man. Funeral at ten."

"May I go up now?"

"Yassuh, you go on up."

He mounted the stairs to the Colonel's room, where they had laid him on the big bed. The shades were drawn, the room was dim and still and stifling. On the white coverlet lay a splendid spray of tuberoses and fern with a heavy fragrance. As he entered, Mrs. Dunham and another neighbor rose silently, touched his shoulder or his hand with grave smiles in passing, and went out, closing the door behind them.

Ridge went slowly to the armchair beside the bed and sat down. He was still there, fasting, when dawn came.

XI

AFTER THE FUNERAL THE NEXT MORNING
the doctor slid his hand through Ridge's arm and said, "You
come along with me."

. Unresisting, he got into the doctor's car, got out at the
office, and submitted patiently to ministrations and inquiry.

"There's nothing wrong with you that regular habits and
steady work and a little peace of mind won't cure," said the
doctor at last. "Where's that girl?"

"Gone back to Massachusetts."

"You haven't contrived to lose her for good, I hope."

"I hope not. But I couldn't ask her to hang around here
on nothing a year while I work this thing out."

"Going to do it the hard way, are you," said the doctor
with approval.

"If I can do it at all. I suppose I couldn't have just one
drink — to sort of kick me upstairs?"

"Certainly you can have a drink." The doctor took a
bottle and a glass from the cupboard and poured a stout
bracer and handed it over. "There's no harm in your taking

[126]

a drink once in a while, when you need it. You're not an alcoholic, Ridge."

"Thanks." He set down the empty glass. "Do you know of anyone who would be willing to go and stay at Fleetwood with my mother at night? Just in case she was taken ill, or had a fall, or something unforeseen. Esther is there to cook, but she's pretty old and likely to lose her head, and of course she doesn't sleep in the house."

"Your mother is as strong as a horse, and anyone I send there will be fired out in no time," said the doctor unsympathetically. "But I'll ask young Abby to go over and try, if you'll be any happier."

"Is she old enough?"

"She's turned sixteen, and is very responsible."

"How time flies," said Ridge. "The last time I noticed Abby she was a toothless pickaninny."

"It would be too much for her mother now. Sarah's getting old, like Esther. But young Abby could cope, if anyone can. She could have a sofa in the upstairs hall to be within call if she was needed."

"Then send her. And furthermore, could you lend me a hundred dollars?"

"I can," said the doctor, and wrote out a check. "When that's gone, let me know."

"When that's gone, things have to be different," said Ridge, and rose. "I'm supposed to go and see Mr. Conway now. And I don't know a subpoena from a search warrant any more."

[127]

"It will come back to you," the doctor said kindly.

Mr. Conway seemed to think it would. He had a stack of papers and books waiting, and spent some time over them with Ridge, and reached satisfactory conclusions. Then he said, "You haven't got transportation, have you, with the Colonel's car smashed up. You can't carry all this stuff back and forth in your arms if you're going to work at home nights. You'll have to have a car of some sort."

"The one at Fleetwood belongs to my mother. She can't drive it but it will have to stay there."

Mr. Conway reached for the telephone and confirmed the whereabouts of something he referred to as the truck. "Fill it up and bring it round here," he said. "Leave it outside my office."

He explained to Ridge that he had taken a small pick-up truck as payment for winning some case or other, where his client was selling out and leaving the county. The only way to realize on it was a third- or fourth-hand sale, if a purchaser could be found. The market for that kind of thing was not very brisk just now. Ridge might as well drive it for the time being — just as a loan, the old lawyer added casually.

Ridge thanked him and a little later went outside to find a disreputable vehicle parked behind Mr. Conway's neat sedan. But it responded to the starter on the third try, and Ridge drove back to Avalon in it, the books and papers on the seat beside him.

They had had the tree and the crushed car removed from

the drive, and the house was looking very much as it had looked ever since he could remember. He felt no satisfaction at possessing it. In acquiring it he had lost his best friend, and all the dearest associations of his youth. He found it necessary to down a sort of dread at the prospect of living here alone among those memories — wondering if he was going to feel himself at best a usurper, for all Jeb's tactful acceptance of the situation, and the old colored man's lifelong affection for the boy who had stood in the place of a son to his master.

And then, as he mounted the steps and entered the bare hall, with its fine stairway sweeping upward, something very mysterious happened. Avalon was not empty or bereft, as he stood there, listening. It awaited him.

There was welcome in the patch of sunlight on the uncarpeted floor at his feet, in the bouquet of fresh flowers visible through the open door of Alice's sitting-room, in the drift of coffee fragrance from the kitchen where Jeb appeared to be getting lunch. The Colonel's body had left it only that morning, with dignity and ceremony. But the essence, the intangible part of the Colonel, his forethought for his only heir, his wry philosophy, his wit and generosity and charity towards all — they were part of the legacy.

Standing uncovered in the hall, his arms full of books and papers which might be his passport to independence and self-respect, Ridge perceived through his pores that he was not alone. In this appalling venture back into realities and responsibilities and reason, no matter how strait the gate, how charged with punishment the scroll, the Colonel would be there to keep him company.

Jeb looked round the dining-room door and saw him standing motionless at the foot of the stairs.

"Got you bite to eat, suh," he said diffidently. "Cain't beat a nice fresh egg, when the soul is sore."

"Thank you, Jeb."

The old colored man took his hat, and Ridge carried his burden into the dining-room with him and laid it on the near end of the vast oval mahogany table. At the opposite end, where the Colonel's chair was, a single place was laid. Ridge walked towards it and paused on the right of it and laid his hand on the back of the chair which stood there.

"This is where I always sit," he said gently. "This is my chair, Jeb."

"Yassuh. Jes' as you say."

He waited while Jeb moved the silver and the place mat and pulled out the chair he had been accustomed to occupy when he shared the Colonel's meager meals. When Mary came back, when he had earned the right, he would take the head of the table.

Jeb watched over him while he ate, so that he dared not leave much on his plate, and as he was about to rise from the table Jeb said anxiously, "Marse Ridge. You ain' got nuffin' to worry about heah, suh. We gots dem hens layin' deyseffs inside out, we gots de truck in de garden, an' dere's sebben dollahs fo'ty-five cents housekeepin' money left outen de pension money. We do all right on dat, suh — we make dat go a long ways, but fo' de likker."

It was his declaration of service to a new master. No further agreement between them was necessary beyond the meeting of eyes. Ridge was touched and grateful, but not surprised.

"We'll manage without the likker," he said quietly.

"I put de bottle in de side-board same as always, suh."

"Yes. All right. Thank you, Jeb." He stood a minute surveying the pile of work on the end of the table. "I think I'll do my writing here," he said. "You leave everything just as you find it, now. Bring a blotter and some pencils and ink. And I'll want an extra lamp."

"Yassuh. Which room you gwine sleep in, suh?"

"The same one I always have," said Ridge. "Air out his room and leave it open, as usual. I want everything just as usual."

"Yassuh. We do dat, suh," said Jeb, with satisfaction.

All through the hot, drowsy afternoon Ridge labored at the work he had brought away from Mr. Conway's office. It was dry, dull, soporific stuff, and more than once his mind wandered to the bottle in the sideboard. When lamp-lighting came, and found it still untouched, he knew his first small victory.

After dinner he went at the papers again, and held to it until long after the hour he usually went to bed with a book to end the long dreariness of the day. On his way towards the stairs with a candle at last, he turned aside and entered Alice's sitting-room. He and the Colonel had often sat there in the evenings with a chess-board between them, or reading aloud, or sometimes he had played Alice's piano, the old tunes the Colonel liked to hear.

He set down the candlestick on the polished top, opened the lid above the keyboard and touched the keys lightly. A dear piano, mellow and true, and the Colonel's main extravagance was to keep it pretty well in tune. He traced a melody in the treble, and then sat down and played with a loving touch the waltz which Chopin wrote because his mistress laughed at her little dog chasing its tail — the waltz that is only a minute long.

But before he reached the final notes Jeb appeared apologetically in the doorway.

" 'Scuse me, suh — Doctor's Abby says kin she speak to you."

"Is she here?" He rose anxiously, and then sat down again, on the piano bench. "Bring her in."

The whites of young Abby's eyes showed in the candle-light.

"Marse Ridge, suh — cain't do no good oveh at yo' place."

"What's the matter?"

"She done throw me out an' lock de do'. She say ef heh own flesh an' blood desert her she don' need nobody else watchin' and spyin' on heh. You tell Doctor I done my best, suh?"

"Yes, I'll tell him. . . . Jeb."

"Yassuh?"

"You know how to drive that truck?"

"I druv de cah, suh."

"All right. Take Abby home, and come straight back here."

"Yassuh."

When they had gone, he sat on, staring down at the keyboard where the "Minute Waltz" had died under his hands. His sense of victory had gone, turned into a conscience-smitten triumph over an old woman who was not quite right in the head, and who was his mother. She had robbed him, as she always could, of any satisfaction or peace of mind. The tug-of-war was on again, her implacable will against his, her unfair advantage, her unfailing theatric sense of how best to turn his words and actions against him so that they would appear mean and malicious, as though he took advantage of a helpless, aging, lonely woman.

"I will not go back," he said aloud, to his own compunctions and wavering determination. "I will not go back to Fleetwood now."

And he took the candle and went up the stairs to the room he had occupied many times before as sanctuary from tempests which raged at home.

Jeb had made it ready for him, even to a lamp beside the bed to read by, and his things were unpacked and put away. But all the time he was undressing, and after he lay with a book open before him, he was thinking, Perhaps if I write to Cousin Flora in Charleston — perhaps I could persuade her to come and stay at Fleetwood, at least for a little while

[133]

— or perhaps Cousin Harriet at Columbia would be better —
she's younger — except that she said last time she would
never come again — who else is there — nobody — everybody's afraid of her now — lucky nobody saw what she did
yesterday — Abby will talk — no one will go near her now,
for love or money — I can't leave her there alone forever —
I won't go back — I won't go back. . . .

XII

You see what happens, Mary told her-self piteously as she drove northward again, feeling empty and thwarted. You see what happens, don't you, when you go back on the General and take up with a real live man. Doesn't make any difference that the General got you into it. If you'd stuck to him you wouldn't be in all this misery now. You always knew where you were, with him. . . .

But something Ridge had taught her, which she had never experienced with the General, flared up inside her rebelliously. I'm glad. If I never saw Ridge again, I'd still be glad. And I will see him. He'll send for me, if I wait long enough. Forever won't be too long, if I get back to Ridge.

But instead of composing letters to Ridge this time as she drove, she was devising what to say at home to explain her sudden return, with no date set and no ring to show — as though he hadn't wanted her, after all. Impossible to prove to them how he had wanted her. . . . The knowledge raced through her again.

She stopped in Baltimore to send off her telegram to

Merriwether, accepting the post for the coming year. She wrote it out with a restive, unresigned sense of eating crow. So where was her handsome hunch now, which had stayed her pen from signing the contract in the first place? Well, yes, he did want to marry her — she acknowledged progress in the warm certainty of his desire. But she might just as well not have made a fool of herself in front of the President and the Head of the History Department that day in the office. A hunch, she decided with unaccustomed irony, is what you want to believe. . . .

"He has just inherited this lovely old house," she explained, sipping lemonade on the porch a few minutes after her arrival at home, while they watched her, one on either side, with anxious, inquisitive faces. She had omitted all mention of the storm and the Colonel's death, which was an experience that belonged to her and Ridge alone. "It will take time and money to get it ready, and — we thought it would be best to wait — "

"A bride usually likes to have some hand in fixing up her own home," Aunt Lucy remarked suspiciously, as though she knew there was something they hadn't been told, or as though she thought Ridge was trying to put something over on the girl he was going to marry.

"I shall have, when the time comes. He hasn't — much money now. We have to have something more in hand. Besides, I — realized I had an obligation to Merriwether. I'm going to save what I can this year, and he's going into a law office in town and do the same."

"You mean you've decided to wait a whole year after all?" her mother asked, sounding faintly scandalized.

Mary was exasperated.

"You were both dead against the idea of my marrying Ridge when I left here!" she cried. "And now it seems as though you're trying to rush me into it!"

Not at all, they said, watching her. But she had seemed so certain when she started out —

"I didn't know about the house, then," she explained lamely. "And I wasn't thinking straight about Merriwether. Besides, his new job will take time. Don't think I would have minded going short for the first year or so," she added hastily. "I would have stayed gladly, and worked it out with him, if that had been practical from either point of view. It was for my sake he wanted to wait."

But by their faces as she went up to unpack her bag and change for dinner she knew what they thought. There was a kind of relief in their faces, and a kind of satisfaction. They thought he had jilted her, or that she had made a mistake. Her cheeks burned.

She attended her first faculty meeting at Merriwether twittering with nerves. There were two other new faculty members besides herself, both of them rather tailored and self-confident. She was standing quietly after the first flurry of introductions, trying to remember names and feeling like a tongue-tied freshman, when a remarkably pleasant male voice at her shoulder said, "Don't look so frightened, you'll get the hang of it."

[137]

Professor Bronson (English Lit) was beside her. His greying hair was a little too long, his eyes were a near-sighted brown, and his shoulders had a literary stoop. She thought frivolously that he was much too much made-up for a fuddy-duddy college prof to get into a Hollywood film, and the smile she gave him was so ready and appealing it made him blink.

"I was feeling a little out of place," she admitted, and "You look a little out of place," he agreed kindly. "But time cures all things. Ten years from now it won't be so notice-able."

They sat down together, and Mary watched the other two being a success and deeply regretted her choice of a teaching career.

When the meeting ended, she and Professor Bronson left the building side by side, and discovered that they were bound in the same direction. She was grateful for his company in her strangeness, but found him a little hard to talk to. Searching for topics of conversation, she noticed a poster advertising the film of *Quo Vadis?* in technicolor, and remarked that she had seen it the night before — add-ing somewhat defiantly that she had been, on the whole, very well entertained.

"I meant to see it myself," he said surprisingly. "But somehow I haven't got round to it. When my wife was alive," the musical, modulated voice went on quite cheer-fully, "we used to see films together quite often. Since she died a few years ago I have gone rather short of such diversions. I feel such a fool going in all by myself," he confided simply.

Mary had a sudden unworthy suspicion that he might be leading up to a suggestion that she keep him company at the box-office, but before she could even wonder what reply she could safely make, he gave her a rather pixie look and added, "I have even gone so far as to contemplate buying a television set, just so that I may be light-minded now and then in the privacy of my own home."

"That is brave of you!" she smiled. "What would Merriwether say to that?"

"I suspect they'd all come sneaking in to look at it," he said. "Anyway, I am convinced that television, like the horseless carriage, is here to stay and we may as well put up with it. I can remember, though you cannot, when the first commercial radios came out. Everyone thought it very infra dig to admit that they listened to those. And if anyone had told me then that within my lifetime the picture as well as the sound could be turned on with a knob, I would have thought them quite demented."

"I'm afraid none of our friends at home have stooped to television yet," Mary confessed.

"Well, I have been reading some of the programs in the newspapers lately," he continued shamelessly. "And I must say some of it looks like very good company. Of course you might think I could just read a book when I want to relax," he went on, almost as though speaking to himself. "But my wife and I always used to read aloud to each other when we had something good. And now the house seems rather too quiet in the evenings, though I have rented the upper floor to two other old fogeys like myself."

"I turn in here," said Mary, and held out her hand in her impulsive, warm-hearted way. "Thank you for being so kind to me on my first day. And good luck to your light-mindedness!"

His slow-dawning smile, his rather peering look of admiration, stayed with her as she went up to her room. Poor dear man, to be so lonely that a television set looked like good company. At least he had not asked her to go to the movies with him, which would have posed a problem in faculty etiquette to which she had as yet no clue.

Things shook down a bit surprisingly soon, and by the second month she had begun to look around her with more confidence. Her classes were going well, and she was no longer nervous about them. She had made a few friends, and instead of being homesick found to her surprise that she enjoyed her new solitude and independence.

Ridge's letters were different now, for he could no longer afford to dream away an afternoon finding phrases to say what she meant to him. He was reading and researching every day in Mr. Conway's extensive legal library, at Mr. Conway's right hand — learning, relearning, and beginning to query and deduce — abstracting deeds and mortgages, preparing contracts of sale, doing most of the leg work for his senior. In the evenings he was teaching himself to use an ancient borrowed typewriter. But if his letters were less lyric they promised something more — they were evidence of a practical, productive state of mind. Still, they gave no inkling of the rugged ups and downs of his daily existence — the mistakes he made, and magnified, the failures, the backsets, the drudgery, the doubting hours, the discouragement and dreary determination to see it through if he died of it now — and the rare, brief moments when he saw, far ahead of him, a glimmer.

X I I I

LEAVING THE HISTORY BUILDING AT THE END
of an October day, Mary encountered Professor Bronson
at the door, and he paused in front of her with his near-
sighted, beaming smile.

"Oh, there you are," he said with satisfaction. "I was
looking for you. I wanted to tell you — I've done it!" He
waited impressively for the light of comprehension which
failed to dawn at once in her surprised face. "I've *got* it!"
he prodded, with an almost boyish urgency. "The television
set!"

"Oh," said Mary hastily, remembering. "How is it? Anything good?"

He gave his sly, pixie look, making her a conspirator in
his downfall.

"I'm afraid I'm going to like it," he said, daring her to
ridicule, and glanced over his shoulder as though for eaves-
droppers. "What's more, certain parties who wouldn't be
caught dead in a ditch with a set in their possession are
beginning to show an unnatural interest in my welfare. The
fact is, I've had more visitors in the past two weeks than
in months before!"

Mary laughed.

"I've heard it works that way," she said.

"So I thought I'd give a party," said Professor Bronson happily. "To sort of introduce it to a few select friends — the ones who jeer the loudest. Will you come?"

"I don't jeer at all!" she denied indignantly.

"Oh, no, I didn't mean that. *You* will help me to defend my Philistine behavior from the more enlightened guests."

"Well, I — I'd love to come and see it sometime," she said hesitantly.

"I'm issuing invitations for Monday night," he said with his youthful enthusiasm. "This too is against an unwritten law, about week-day entertaining. But I have to choose the night by the program, instead of obliging the audience to enjoy whatever entertainment may be provided on a Friday or Saturday evening. I chose this Monday," he added in a rather personal tone, "because the play is a period piece. I thought you would find it interesting, if only to tell us what they did wrong."

"I shall come to enjoy myself, not to criticize," said Mary.

"O rare and delightful woman!" he cried, making it sound like a quotation. "How they could all learn from you! Eight o'clock, please. Refreshments will be served."

He took himself off, looking pleased and near-sighted and naughty.

Dean Sanderson had an unusually loud voice with a pene-trating quality. Mary arrived at Professor Bronson's house

[143]

on Monday evening in time to hear it saying, "But you've changed everything in the room all round! You haven't anywhere to sit!"

"I have exactly the same number of chairs I always had, but they are all over there," Professor Bronson replied, unruffled. "Good evening, Miss Carmichael. I believe you know everyone here."

The new television set, a modest table model, occupied a position of prominence at one end of the room, and it was true that the furniture had been rearranged to face it. It was turned on, with the sound cut down, so that the figures moved and grimaced in pantomime, like an old silent film. Mary joined a knot of people standing in front of it pretending in a rather supercilious way to be amused.

"That program is of no importance," Professor Bronson remarked without concern. "I'm just warming up the set. But I'll ask you to make yourselves comfortable, please, before the real show begins. There is plenty of time. Miss Carmichael — " With playful formality he indicated a chair for Mary. "This will be right up your alley, as it has an historical theme. . . ."

People began to choose their seats, with the usual unselfish determination to sit at the back or on the side, and there was the usual discussion about how much light there should be in the room.

Mary sat uncomfortably where he had placed her, dreading the obligation to render judgment. If she found fault with the production she spoiled Professor Bronson's innocent fun. If she defended and praised it, she was convicted of his own childish susceptibility to a new toy, and would be patronized accordingly.

She decided in favor of pleasing her host, whatever the cost, and then was rewarded by an hour's sensible entertainment which only a hypercritical audience could have wholly condemned. The material which followed was not as good, and attention soon wandered into whispering and movement, and somebody turned on more lights. An elderly maid began to hand round sandwiches, and there was the convivial clink of ice in tumblers.

Mary found herself the center of a small group which had somehow got her to talking about the Southern trip she had made in search of her lost General. They were genuinely interested, and she forgot to be shy. Miss Peterson, who was one of the tailored ones, was from North Carolina herself, and was inclined to cross-examine. Miss Mason, whose family lived in the right part of Boston, had a brother who went South for the wild turkey shooting whenever he got a chance — he was in the Army now — and always stayed at a plantation run by two dear old ladies (who proved not to be the Sibley girls, though they also took paying guests in a genteel way with a thumping bill at the end). A lot of Southern families, said Miss Mason with authority, lived all year on the proceeds of the paying-guest season during hunting. The rates charged at those places were really fantastic, but the customers felt it was worth it, to step out of this world however briefly into an illusion of life as people used to live it in a nearly forgotten era of leisure and charm.

When the evening ended, Mary had been a success herself and so had Professor Bronson's television set, although everyone agreed that he had stacked the cards by picking a program which was the exception rather than the average. Professor Bronson bridled at this, and said Very well, come any time — just come for pot luck any time, and see what they found.

A couple of weeks later Miss Mason rang Mary's phone and invited her for a week-end at the Mason home in Boston.

"I won't pretend it's not sudden," she said frankly, "though I would have got round to it very soon anyway. My brother is up from Washington unexpectedly for a few days and he brought a friend with him, and I want an extra girl."

"Oh, a blind date," said Mary.

"Well, not exactly, it's my own brother I'm asking you for, you're not taking much of a risk," Miss Mason replied, sounding a trifle nettled.

"It's very kind of you," said Mary hastily. "But I think I ought to warn you I'm no good at bridge."

"Well, that's all right, we're not a card-playing family. My brother Alec has been South a good deal, you know, for the shooting — so you'll have lots to talk about. I finish early on Fridays, so I'm going in on the train. I'll have Alec pick you up here on Saturday morning, in time for lunch with us. He drives a blue Cadillac rather recklessly, and you'll know him by the stars on his shoulders, and three rows of ribbons on his chest. You're an angel to come. Good-bye."

The receiver clicked.

Oh, no, not a general! Mary thought helplessly, and in desperation began to wonder what she could come down with before Saturday and not have to go.

XIV

Saturday was upon her before she had been able to invent any plausible excuse, and she had anyway begun to view the relentless acceleration of her quiet life with something like resignation. Ever since she had first set out for Carolina last April things had been happening to her. The graph had shot skywards and she seemed powerless in its flight. She had once been one of those people nothing ever happened to. Then, merely by entering her General's one-time orbit, she was apparently caught in the backwash of his dynamic after course, and swept into emotions and contingencies impossible to anticipate or retard. And now, because she had talked too much at Professor Bronson's party and so called Miss Mason's attention to herself, she was being picked up by a reckless blue Cadillac with a general's stars.

When he came, she was ready, wearing sober navy blue and white with a Dutch cap on her soft, shining hair, and just a touch of pink lipstick on her shy, curled-up smile.

In the first place, he was enormous, after the fashion of

a University fullback, which he had been in his not-too-distant day. He loomed in the doorway above her, an ex-combat man, young for his rank, filling his uniform as though it had grown on him, with a dark, sardonic face which now registered flabbergasted pleasure.

"*Well!*" said Miss Mason's brother Alec, without pre-liminaries. "Or have I come to the wrong door?"

"I'm Mary Carmichael. And you've got the stars and the ribbons. We can't be two other people."

"I require a little orientation," said Alec. "I understood them to say that you teach history here."

"I do."

"I went to the wrong school," he said. "Your bags ready?"

She showed him a single suitcase, standing just inside the door.

"Is that all?" he asked, with a glance round.

"Yes, I — didn't think I'd need a trunk for two days."

"Light of my life, where have you been?" said Alec rhetorically, and led the way to the car. "No hat-box," he marvelled. "No shoe-bag. No dressing-case-with-bottles, weighing roughly a ton. No anything-that-wouldn't-go-in-at-the-last-minute. A suitcase — " He set it reverently in the back of the car. "Her hat on, her smile on, she walks out the door in nothing flat. You know, you'd make some man a wonderful wife!" He closed the door on her care-fully, as though a jar might break her, walked around the car and slid under the wheel. "I've been out of circulation

[149]

too long," he said. "They didn't do things this way when I left."

"How long have you been away?" she asked politely, as the car shot away from the curb.

"Except for six months back in 1946, after the war, I've been overseas since 1943. Now it looks as though I'm due for a nice long stretch in Washington, God help me."

"I haven't known many soldiers," Mary said. "What part of the Army are you in?"

"She hasn't known many soldiers," said Alec softly, to the wheel. "How does a girl *not* know soldiers these days? The woods are full of 'em."

"No one can believe that you can live with your mother and your aunt in a glass case," said Mary.

"Was that what you did?"

"Even while I went to college. Even while I worked for my M.A. I can see now that it was a mistake."

"Well, I don't know," said Alec, his big brown hands relaxed and easy on the wheel while the speedometer climbed. "It gives you a certain Something."

"I'm afraid it does," she sighed.

"You're cute," said Alec, with approval. "Sally is smarter than I thought she was."

It was a cryptic remark which he never elucidated.

The Masons lived in one of those imposing houses in Louisburg Square. Feeling like a country cousin, Mary stood in the great hall being made welcome by Miss Mason, whose name, of all things, was Sally, and her almost too gracious mother, with piled white hair and a bosom.

"Hi, Mack," said Alec to a fourth figure in the background. "Look what I found."

Mack advanced to be introduced – a red-head and a mere captain.

"Does it really teach history at a girls' college?" he asked, forgetting to let go Mary's hand.

"It's got an M.A.," said Alec, awed.

"Well, dawgone," said Mack, and "Boys!" said Sally briskly. "Lay off that. Miss Carmichael – may we call you Mary? – isn't going to fall for any such line as that."

"Still got her milk teeth," said Mack, as Mary recovered her hand. "It don't seem right to catch 'em so young and stick M.A.'s on 'em."

"Very funny," said Sally, who had her Ph.D. "Come along, Mary, if you want to wash up before lunch."

"Don't lose her," Alec cautioned as the two girls started up the staircase. "My life has just begun."

"What on earth have you done to Alec?" Sally asked as they reached Mary's room, where her suitcase had preceded them. "He hasn't shown any signs of life for months, you ought to have a medal."

"Was he wounded?"

"Not recently. He's getting over a divorce."

"Oh," said Mary.

"It wasn't his fault," Sally remarked, very offhand to cover the fact that it mattered to her a very great deal what people thought of Alec. "I'm not saying that because I'm his sister. She really was a so-and-so. But he took it very hard."

"I'm sorry," said Mary, inadequately, she felt.

"Well, just do what you can do to cheer him up. He's sort of through with women." Sally turned at the door. "We're going to the game, did I tell you? Don't bother to change, I'll lend you a warmer coat."

Harvard won, so dinner was festive. There were six couples to a sit-down meal, and a dozen more came in later. A large room suddenly opened up at the back with a Capehart in it — no television — and Mary's heart sank again as a few of them began to dance.

"Come on," said Alec, reaching for her, and "It's one of those Spanish rhythms," she complained, holding back. "I don't know the step."

"It's simple — I'll teach you."

"Oh, but — "

But she was on the polished floor, his arm around her waist, distractedly doing as he told her — her head came barely to his chin, his body was hard and warm inside the close-cut uniform, with its metallic masculine accessories, his breath was on her cheek — very soon the beat and pulse of the samba caught her and she was following his strong, simple lead without thinking about her feet.

"You're wonderful," said Alec against her hair. "Let me teach you some more things."

It was after midnight when Mary reached her room

again, and she had drunk a glass of champagne — well, a glass and a refill. It was her first champagne, and her first public conquest. She sat down on the edge of her bed and stared into space, still wearing her evening dress, still breathing rather fast.

What had happened? Something had, she didn't need a mirror to tell her that. A year ago Alec would not have given her a rush like this. Was it because of Ridge and the banked fires he had kindled? A woman in love has a shine and a softness and a light within. And she was in love with Ridge. He had done this for her, he had made her desirable to other men by his own desire. She owed it all to Ridge — even her first beau.

She tipped over on the bed, fully dressed, and laid her hot cheek against the turned-down sheet. It was just Alec's way, to make a fuss of a woman. He didn't mean half he said. And yet — ought she to mention Ridge somehow, before it went any further? You couldn't just say, "Look out, I'm engaged." And besides, she wasn't engaged. If you see anything better, Ridge had said, take it and be happy. As though she would. As though she would trade Ridge for a dozen Alecs. What would the General think?

The word took her unawares. Alec's stars. General Mason, he was, after all. So now she had another one. And they were very much alike, she thought, flung down on the bed in the dress she had danced in. It was a coincidence. But Alec's headlong ways must be very like the other's methods with the Tory girl who could not bear to see him caught by her own people. Alec was the kind of man she had always dreamed of, the kind to carry a woman clean off her feet, the darling-of-the-gods type. Before she saw Ridge. Now Alec was too late.

She rose, a little crumpled, and undressed slowly and got into bed, and on account of the champagne fell asleep with the bedside light on.

Breakfast was English-style, with hot plates on the sideboard and people coming down when they felt like it.

Mary was late, partly because she had slept so tight, and partly because then she had dawdled, unwilling to face the situations implicit in the day before her. Therefore everybody but Mrs. Mason was in the dining-room when she appeared, and she was lovingly plied with food. She wondered about church, but it seemed not to occur to anybody else, so she kept a cowardly silence on that. Alec sat next to her, half-turned in his chair, smoking and watching her eat, for he had finished.

"You look as though you had slept," he said with his habitual air towards her of wonder and disbelief.

"I did."

"You would!"

"Didn't you?"

There was a long pause, and she noticed that Sally and Mack had left the table and were squabbling over the Sunday papers near the window. Alec brooded at her.

"I had things to think about," he said, and waited for

her to ask what things. "One of your chief charms in a jaded world," he continued when she didn't, "is the way you never pick up a cue."

She glanced round at him, with scrambled eggs in her mouth.

"What was I supposed to say then?" she asked, when she decently could.

Alec gave a sort of grunt of laughter.

"Don't ever let 'em make a schoolmarm out of you," he said. "It would be such a waste."

Mary bristled becomingly.

"Are you one of those men who think women's place is in the home?"

"It depends on the woman." His sombre eyes rested audaciously on her face. "I'd hate to see you get like Sally."

"I wish I *was* like her!"

"There are lots of them like her." He brushed them aside. "They're all right, I guess — till you come along and make us remember a lot of things we had forgotten. Say What things," he prodded, as she was silent. "Or do you know perfectly well what I'm talking about, behind that innocent face of yours? That's what you've got — innocence. And by God, I believe it's real!"

"If you two have finished stuffing yourselves," said Sally behind them, "how about driving out to the club for some tennis and lunch?"

Mary raised a stricken face.

[155]

"I'm no good at tennis," she said, and Mack hooted with affectionate laughter.

"Ready to be shot at sunrise, because she's 'no good at tennis,' " he quoted in a panicked falsetto. "Baby, you don't have to be good at tennis. You just sit there, with all your dear little clothes on, and your funny little face on, and you will not be alone."

"I can guarantee it," said Alec. "Haven't had a racquet in my hand for years."

They went to the club, and Sally and Mack played tennis, and both of them were very good at it indeed, though Sally was tactless enough to take two sets from him. Mary and Alec sat at the side of the court and watched, and a great many people came and went, greeting Alec with cordial surprise and getting themselves introduced to his companion.

They lunched in a crowd of the Masons' friends, and then watched more tennis, and then it was drink time. Tom Collinses appeared, Scotch-and-sodas, Old-fashioneds — Alec ordered a brown sherry for Mary, and it came in a little lily-shaped glass and she made it last while everybody else had a second round. They got home just in time to change for dinner, and while Sally appeared in a different creation Mary simply wore the same blue and white dress she had worn the night before, because she had brought only one.

The party was smaller that night, and after dinner they broke up into groups in the big drawing-room. Alec took

Mary and their coffee to a small table in a corner and turned his shoulder on the rest of the company.

"I've got to catch a plane in an hour," he said. "I want to see you again, please. You do something to me. Are you booked up at Christmas time? I might get away again then."

"I shall have to go home, I'm afraid. They're expecting me."

"Where is home?"

She told him.

"Could I come to see you there?"

Mary was startled.

"Oh, *no* — that is — they wouldn't know what to think."

"Who are They?"

"My mother and my aunt."

"Am I going too fast for you?" he asked with amusement. "It's a way we have in the Army, being always pressed for time."

"But they think — you see, there's a man down South — "

"Is there? What sort of man? Are you engaged to him?" He glanced at her left hand, which was bare.

"N-no, he — "

"That's his hard luck, then," said Alec, rather grimly.

"But we're in love," she got out, with some desperation. "It's just that he hasn't any money. He has to have a little time — "

"Tell me about him, will you? It's not idle curiosity," said Alec, setting down his coffee cup. "I'd like to know where I am on this thing."

She found it difficult, and she told it badly, and her audience was prejudiced.

"I know the type," he said unsympathetically. "One of those aristocratic bums. Family mansion — hereditary glamor — sweet potato accent — drinks a bit on the side — the you-are-my-salvation line. Don't you fall for it, sweetheart, you're much too nice a girl to spend the rest of your life in genteel poverty with a charming souse. And they can be charming, I know that. But don't."

"You're not being fair!" Mary cried angrily. "You can't just reduce Ridge to the lowest common denominator without even seeing him! You've got no right to assume — "

"Mary, I know that country, I've spent a lot of time down there," he argued patiently. "Mind you, I love it, it's nostalgic and picturesque, and it gets hold of you. But even if I weren't falling in love with you, I'd hate to see you marry into it!"

"I'd have done that already if he hadn't made me wait till he proved he could earn a living," she said defiantly.

"Good for him. A man would have to be pretty much of a heel to take advantage of a girl like you. How long do you expect to wait for him?"

"Till he sends for me. He's gone to work in a law office."

"One of those gentlemen's jobs."

"He *is* a gentleman!"

"Sure, sure, they all are. Well, this is where I should bow myself out and mind my own business, and let you throw your life away," said Alec with a long sigh. "But before

[158]

I do that I'm going to make one more squawk. So you wait for him. How long? While your best years go by, and I get back into a shooting war again, and then what's left for us, you and me. Now I've scared hell out of you, haven't I. And I've said more than I meant to tonight. I don't expect you to make up your mind about me as fast as this — I'm used to making quick decisions, and with a soldier it's always later than you think. Sally probably told you, I've been over the jumps, I know the score. But you — all of a sudden, I believe in Santa Claus again." He touched her hand briefly, with just the tip of his forefinger drawn along it. "Don't worry about it, sweetheart. But you haven't told me anything yet to make me give up. I'll be seein' you." He rose, erect and splendid in the fitted uniform. "Mack. What's the time?"

X V

THERE WAS A LETTER FROM RIDGE AWAIT-
ing her when she got back to her quiet room at Merriwether. He made a very funny story of his first case —
Mr. Conway had given him a chance, in fact had insisted
that it was time for him to plead a case — a farmer who had
lent a friend $55 and then, the loanee having suffered a sad
loss of memory, the lender had sued to collect his debt. De-
fendant had been unable to account otherwise for his possession of sufficient ready cash to make certain traceable
purchases at that time — it appeared that he had simply put
his hand in his pocket and pulled it out full of money he
had had no idea was there. When asked if such miracles
were a common occurrence with him, he at first became
very deaf, and then conceded that he hadn't ever had exactly the same experience before. Plaintiff had not required
of him an IOU but had produced at the trial a mutual acquaintance who went into total recall and described the
circumstances of the loan at great length. . . .

Mary laughed at the story, noted the progress to court
activity, and read the letter again for love, and found it

rather restrained. She did not know that it had been written on the end of the dining-room table after a long evening copying out abstracts and legal correspondence, when Ridge's vital spark had run very low, and a feeling of faint disappointment lingered with her as she sat down to answer it. It was not the way he used to write.

Pen in hand, she debated the wisdom of making her own story of the week-end, and how it must be all thanks to him that people courted her now, so that it didn't matter about not playing bridge and tennis, since he had brought her alive and made her prettier, as even she could see for herself. But then she decided that that sounded like bragging, and because for the first time she was withholding something from him, her letter came out a little stilted and unspontaneous. And the slow attrition that usually attacks a correspondence sooner or later had begun.

A few days before the Christmas holidays, Professor Bronson appeared at the door of her classroom just as she was closing up to go home. The students had all departed from the room, and he had obviously chosen his time. He laid a small parcel, wrapped discreetly in ordinary brown paper and tied with white string, on her desk, and said in his melancholy, musical tones, "Santa Claus seems to have left this with me by mistake — I thought I had better deliver it for him."

She was touched and a little embarrassed, as it had not occurred to her to provide a gift for him. There had been a few more television parties, a few chance encounters, but that was all. Making conversation, she inquired his Christmas plans, and learned that his two elderly lodgers would be away and that he faced a completely solitary holiday in the too-quiet house. She was leaving the next day to spend the vacation at home, and something about his utter lack of self-pity or expectation wrung her heart, so that she said impulsively, "Why don't you drive down with me tomorrow and spend Christmas with us — if you can bear a houseful of women?"

She saw the flash of pure delight cross his face before his good manners and his habitual self-depreciation extinguished it.

"That's very kind of you," he said punctiliously with real gratitude, "but I doubt if your family would be pleased to have a total stranger on their hands for such an intimate time as Christmas."

"You're not altogether a stranger to them," she told him kindly. "They have already met you in my letters."

He looked at her wistfully, longing to believe the good fortune of her invitation.

"If you think they wouldn't find it rather short notice — " he began with a visible weakening of resolution.

"Of course not," she said stoutly, against her own qualms. "I'll phone them tonight. The guest-room is always ready and very seldom used. I'm planning to start tomorrow morning about ten. Would that be convenient for you, if I call for you with the car?"

"Quite convenient," he assented, still hesitant, not meeting her eyes. "I must confess, last year was rather dreadful," he added. "I was wondering how to face it again."

"Well, you don't have to," said Mary decisively. "Just you throw some things into a bag and come along with me."

"Thank you." He raised his honest, peering look. "I had no idea when I came here — " He gestured vaguely towards the parcel which had brought him. "I mean, I wasn't — "

"Why, of course not! But I would have suggested it sooner if I had known you were going to be alone," she protested, touched by his defenceless simplicity. "We're rather too quiet ourselves on holidays, I think. I'll be outside your door tomorrow at ten."

He went away still murmuring his thanks, and — "Now, *how* did I get myself into that!" she said to herself with misgivings which went on growing as she put in her long-distance call to announce their guest at home.

Her mother was surprised, but made no objections. The room would be ready, she said. There was plenty to eat. They would find some suitable little gifts for him before he arrived.

It was not a long drive, but even so the conversation flagged more than once, though his gratitude and pleasure did not, and she found herself longing for reinforcements in the shape of family small talk. Fortunately she would not have to deal with it alone again till the return drive, and by then there would be more common ground established by the visit.

He was received warmly into the household life by her

family — so warmly, so like an old friend, that Mary wondered a little, and then laid it to the obvious fact that he was their kind of man, and comprehensible to them — as Ridge would not have been, with his mysterious background of idleness and Southern glamor, or (God forbid!) Alec in his arrogant masculine magnetism.

By the end of the first evening she had begun to suspect still another reason for their cordiality, to which Professor Bronson was responding with unexpected gallantry towards all concerned — perhaps her family had some idea that he might cut Ridge out, and make her forget her Carolina madness. It was on the face of it a ludicrous idea, but as time went on she saw much evidence to support it. They were accepting this dear, harmless old fuddy-duddy in order to be rid of the unknown Southern menace and what they could only regard as an infatuation which perhaps had now run its course. By Christmas Day she was reduced to hoping only that Professor Bronson was too near-sighted and naïf to catch on, himself, to an increasingly noticeable conspiracy to annex him as a permanent member of the family.

Christmas morning was enlivened by the arrival of two dozen incredible red roses, sent by wire from Washington with a perfectly dead-pan card from General A. V. L. Mason enclosed. Mary, who had never received flowers from a man before, let alone red roses, was nonplussed almost to tears, but at the same time acknowledged the warm, spreading thrill which no woman can deny at such a gift.

In the astounded family silence which accompanied the rustle of green tissue paper as she lifted out into her arms this most incriminating tribute, her Aunt Lucy said in a thin, cold voice, "Isn't that just like a man! He's put a week's earnings into flowers!"

"They're not from Ridge," Mary had to say, which produced a still more resounding pause. "They're from a man I met on that week-end in Boston," she blurted, feeling rather hot in the cheeks. "We went to the football game. He just — he's just the kind that sends flowers, he's very well off, apparently — " She buried her face against the cool petals. "I really never expected to hear from him again."

She felt through the back of her head the glance which passed between her mother and her aunt.

An hour later came Ridge's telegram: A MERRIER CHRISTMAS NEXT YEAR TOGETHER MY LOVE RIDGE — which was the nearest thing to a proposal she had had from him yet.

"It's from Ridge," she had to explain, and put it back in the envelope without showing it to them. "Merry Christmas, and so forth."

Professor Bronson's gift to her proved to be a slim historical volume, exquisitely printed and illustrated, which with great foresight and care he had ordered for her from England weeks ago.

He insisted on returning home the day after Christmas, in his fear of trespassing on their good will, and as the weather was fine Mary drove him back, and conversation was, as she had anticipated, much freer this time. She was congratulating herself on having brought the whole thing off rather well, when he said, "We are almost there. I must thank you, my dear, for the happiest day I have had in years."

"I'm glad," said Mary, wondering with renewed pity how long he had lived alone, after all.

"I have no idea why you should be so kind to me — "

"You were kind to me, that awful first day — remember?"

"That was nothing. You looked so young and vulnerable, I couldn't bear it." He laid his gloved hand for a moment on hers on the wheel. "Forgive me — but I couldn't help noticing the roses. May I ask — are you perhaps engaged to him?"

"Oh, no, not to him!" Mary denied hastily, taking fright at the idea of any such rumor reaching Sally Mason by some roundabout, unauthorized way and creating an uncomfortable situation for everybody. "I can't think what made him burst out like that with such a — *flattering* gift! He knows perfectly well that the man I'm — practically engaged to is in South Carolina. I met him on that trip I told you about."

"You say practically engaged," said Professor Bronson thoughtfully, his eyes on the road. "Does that mean you haven't quite made up your mind?"

"Oh, we've both made up our minds," said Mary, innocent of any necessity to head off whatever he might be going to say next, but instinctively accomplishing that end.

[166]

"But first he wants to prove that he can earn a living at law."

"Not very easy these days, I'm afraid," said Professor Bronson after a moment, very quietly.

"No — I'm afraid not," she sighed. "Of course it's very upsetting to my family — because of his being a total stranger to them, and all that. But you'd think they'd be glad, wouldn't you, that he wants a good income before marrying — instead of which they act as though there was something *suspicious* about it! I don't really know how to handle it, sometimes," she finished pathetically, succumbing to a lonely need for counsel from so unobtrusive and helpful a listener.

And the only thing he had to offer her himself, he was thinking, was whatever security there might still be in the world as it was today. That probably wouldn't sound very exciting to her now, and he could not bring himself to mention it, in the face of the competition. He wanted her to know. He thought a woman had the right to know, when anybody felt about her the way he was beginning to feel about Mary, even though the circumstances were such that nothing could ever come of it. If Mary went on teaching at Merriwether a few more years — but she wouldn't, a girl like Mary was bound to go, before long, to some new life of her own. It would only trouble her, he felt, if he added the tactless burden of his own middle-aged devotion to her already complicated problem. If somehow the others failed her — if by some miracle she decided against both of them — if ever she wanted a haven. . . . It was a remote

[167]

but desperate dream. But if ever Mary needed something none of the younger men could provide . . .

He touched her hand again, briefly.

"If ever I can be of any use, even just as a wailing-wall," he said, "don't hesitate to let me know."

"Thank you," said Mary, with a bright and grateful glance. "You can see now what they are at home. Just grown-up children. I have to — work things out for myself, always."

"Come and talk to me if you feel like it," he said, striving to sound impersonal and elderly. "Sometimes someone outside the family is easier to take advice from. Not that I would presume to give advice," he corrected himself hastily, "but sometimes just to talk out loud helps."

"Oh, yes, sometimes I think it would," she agreed fervently. "I'll remember that, and take you up on it some day."

X V I

THE NOTE SHE WROTE TO ALEC TO THANK
him for the roses was the result of many false starts and was
a little masterpiece of diplomacy and slightly formal friendship. After all, he had kept silence for nearly two months.
And then *boom*.

He laughed when he read it, and reached for his pen and
a sheet of very official notepaper.

ANGEL-FACE [he wrote in a black flowing scrawl]:
You thought I had forgotten, didn't you, but I was
only biding my time and working out logistics. Sally and
I have evolved quite a sound scheme. Your Easter vacation comes early this year — in March. How would it be
if you and Sally jumped in a plane and came down to
Washington for a few days? There's plenty to do here,
and I could arrange to get a little time off. Don't say No.
Love,

ALEC

So Sally was in it too. Mary contemplated the idea in
what she considered a very detached and sensible way,
while a secret, half-formed plan of her own to run back

[169]

to Ridge for even one day at Easter time stood by resolutely in the back of her mind. Not till I send for you, he had said. But that meant for keeps. Surely there wasn't any law against just a day or two along the way, if only as a sort of anniversary, if only as encouragement. . . . Should she ask him first? Or should she just go. . . ?

Then Sally was on the telephone. Alec's timing was perfect.

"About our Easter holiday," Sally was saying confidently. "Don't you think it's a marvellous idea?"

"Well, I — "

"It's an opportunity that I for one wouldn't miss," Sally went on happily. "Even apart from the fact that Alec will turn the town inside out for you, he has a sweet little house in Georgetown and a real Southern cook, and gives heavenly parties."

"I don't think I — well, I haven't got the right clothes for a trip like that," Mary objected futilely.

"Buy some, stupid! I'll come along with you and tell you what. You won't have any other expenses, we'll be staying with Alec in Georgetown."

"No, I can't, really, I — had other plans."

"I bet I know," said Sally. "You were going back to Carolina."

"Y-yes, I was." She had never quite admitted it before.

"But you've been to Carolina. You owe it to yourself, if not to Alec, to see Washington too."

Mary wanted to scream that she didn't owe Alec any-

[170]

thing, and that a day with Ridge would be worth a week in Washington, but held desperately to her manners. Sally took her silence for a weakening of purpose towards Carolina, and said, "Well, anyway, we've got several weeks to talk you into it. Don't go and commit yourself to anything else, will you."

It was very clever of them. And they honestly meant it for her own good, honestly believing that she should be rescued, however ruthlessly, from throwing herself away on a ne'er-do-weel Southerner who would never take the proper care of her. It was interfering and snobbish of them too, but they came of a class which has no inferiorities or doubts about itself, and does not let I-dare-not wait upon I-would. Alec's rather world-weary spirit sensed the strength and sweetness of hers if it could be roused to his need, and Sally, who loved her brother dearly, was only thankful to see him showing signs of life again, and if Mary Carmichael was what he wanted Sally was ready to help him win her any way she could.

XVII

R<small>IDGE, WALKING PERILOUSLY A NARROW</small> way between achievement and despair, seldom allowed himself the luxury of writing a love letter now. By the end of the day his brain was fagged and his writing arm was cramped, and his thoughts would wander wilfully towards the bottle in the sideboard, which he kept there as a necessary part of his probation. The sheer physical effort of gathering his forces and holding to his strenuous schedule was staggering, and sometimes he moved in a haze of fatigue into a sort of fourth dimension or second wind, in which he did some of his best work and clearest thinking. He stayed at concert pitch and dared not come unstrung. And if his thoughts wandered also towards the Easter vacation, he was careful not to mention it. Not quite yet. . . .

As soon as he had got things a little in hand he had paid a visit to Cousin Flora in Charleston. If he was going to be a lawyer he might as well get some experience by pleading his own case with her.

She lived in a small, charming house on the correct side of Broad Street, where for many years, herself a spinster, she had kept house for an eccentric bachelor uncle, who left her the house and a competence when he died. But he took with him the companionship and responsibility on which she had built her busy, contented life. "Cousin Flora's lost her job," the family said sadly, after the funeral, and they took turns inviting her to come and stay, and everyone was very kind to her, and because she was naturally good company and disdained self-pity in any form, she was most welcome wherever she went and could have spent the rest of her life on a continuous round of visits if she had cared to live that way.

But after a few months Cousin Flora returned to the house in Charleston, cleaned it from top to bottom, reappeared at church, asked people in to tea and little dinners, accepted invitations, and generally resumed her life as nearly as possible as though Uncle Thad had not died at all, but had just stepped out to buy some cigars and would be back in time for dinner. It was a wise and courageous thing to attempt, and she succeeded very well in maintaining the illusion that the absence of the one being around whom her world had revolved was only temporary.

Seated in her parlor drinking China tea from shallow, translucent porcelain, listening to her amusing flow of chatter, Ridge felt his heart and purpose fail him. She was so cosy here, so unafflicted and serene. Uncle Thad, for all his fabulous charm and the brilliance of his conversation, must have been rather a handful for twenty-four hours a day every day. It was too much to ask of her now, that having survived the rigors of some thirty years of Uncle Thad and reached so snug a harbor, she should undertake the joyless task of keeping the lid on at Fleetwood. He could not bring himself to suggest such a thing.

He therefore sat rather silent but attentive, feeling all his determination and persuasion ooze out of him, when she said, with the habitual tartness which disguised a very soft heart, "Cat got your tongue, Ridge?"

He smiled at her with deep affection, and she waited for him to explain, for she felt she had been left in the dark long enough as to the reason for his visit, his unusually prosperous appearance, and his unexpected sortie into the world he had practically renounced some years before.

"I was thinking," he admitted, and his glance took in the comfortable room, "how very well off you are here, all by yourself."

"All by myself," she repeated. "That's the only catch in it."

"Do you get lonely, then?"

"Sometimes. But don't tell anybody, they'd all start being good to me, and I couldn't bear that. You see, I'd got used to having somebody to look after. Now nobody makes me any trouble at all, and I find it rather dull. I suppose you wouldn't care to come and live here and be a nuisance in my old age?"

It was a shrewd guess, even though it was the wrong one, and he was touched.

"That's a very flattering offer," he said. "And I haven't

much doubt I could manage the nuisance part, though perhaps not on quite the same scale as Uncle Thad."

"Oh, well, he had a real knack for it," she conceded. "No doubt you'd get the hang of it as you went along."

They laughed together and he reached out a hand to her across the table, and she laid hers in it, warmly.

"Cousin Flora, the truth is, I want to get married."

"It's high time," she agreed, covering her surprise. "Anybody special, or are you just shopping round?"

"Somebody very special," he said, and was thereupon hypnotized into telling all about Mary and the General and the night at Avalon and the break with his mother and the job in Mr. Conway's office. "I came here to ask a tremendous favor of you," he finished. "But now that I realize how tremendous it would be, I don't ask it after all. I must find some other way."

"You want me to go and stay with Fanny at Fleetwood," she said.

"Yes, I did. But I can't ask you to give up all this — tranquillity — for the sort of life you would have to put up with there. Nor I don't ask you to bring her here, even if she would come. It wouldn't be — fitting, for her to be in Charleston now."

Cousin Flora glanced round the quiet room, much as he had done a few minutes before. It was infinitely precious to her, but it was empty too. Empty not only of a presence, but of a need. Except the need which had come into it with Ridge.

"You'd be a lot easier in your mind, wouldn't you, if I was there with her."

"Well, yes, but I — "

"Somebody ought to be with her."

"Somebody has to be. I've let her try it alone because she wouldn't let Abby stay, and she won't have Esther in the house at night. I thought she might have to give in — a cold, or — just the loneliness. But she's tougher than I am. She can bear it, but I can't. She's sat me out and won, as usual. It can't go on like this much longer, something will have to be done."

"I'd better go up there and have a sniff round," said Cousin Flora, and he looked at her with mingled gratitude and guilt.

"I ought to be shot for asking it of you."

"You didn't ask it."

"You didn't give me time."

"Some day, Ridge, your conscience is going to kill you."

"I hope to outlive it," he smiled. "How about your own?"

She shook her head.

"It's not my conscience that takes me to Fleetwood," she said. "Nor just my love for you, Ridge. I have been idle and easy long enough here. It's never felt natural to me. I like to be *doing* something, and if coping with Fanny Creston is my next job I reckon I'm ready for it. I don't have as much trouble with her as most people do, you know — I don't care a pin for her tantrums, and she can't work on my sympathy or make me angry, either one. May I have the pink bedroom?"

"My dear Cousin Flora, you may have anything in my power to give you, including the pink bedroom!"

"It gets the morning sun," she said. "And the moonrise. And now that you've got electricity I can have my little radio by the bed." Her eyes went again around her own familiar drawing-room, which suddenly looked very peaceful and a bit forlorn, as though it knew it was going to be left, and for a moment she wished she need not go, knowing only too well the Spartan comfort which prevailed at Fleetwood. It was true enough that she often felt lost without someone to make endless, fretful demands on her time and good temper. But at the same time it was possible to have a little too much of a good thing, and life at Fleetwood would carry things pretty far in that direction. Only for Ridge could she undertake so cheerless a task — but Ridge would thank her all his life, and Ridge's wife too, if he were set free now by anything so simple as her giving up this snug idleness of hers to take on a full-size job again. It was the least one could do for Ridge, who was looking better than she had ever thought to see him look again, and was still young, with a life to make. . . . "I shall be very cosy there, and I'll get in a bit of gardening too, and see if I can't bring those japonicas back to what they used to be," she went on, reassuring herself as well as Ridge that things need not be so bad. "Some day you may want to live there again yourself."

[177]

Ridge went down on one knee and put his arms around her in her chair.

"You aren't fooling me, you know," he said gently. "*Or* yourself. We both know what you're giving up, for me. But I shan't be far away, and I promise I'll always do my very best to be a nuisance to you in my own way."

XVIII

To PROFESSOR BRONSON'S KIND, NEAR-sighted eyes it was soon apparent that something was wrong with Mary. She was not noticeably thin or pale, she was simply toned down, as though the light inside her was flickering instead of burning bright.

He gave her several opportunities, but she kept to herself with a pitiful stubbornness, and he had a horror of prying. The fourth time he deliberately placed himself in her way her eyes rested on him with a new speculation, and she said rather suddenly, "Would you have time to go for a drive with me? My car is just over there."

"Why, yes — I could go for a drive," he answered, pretending surprise, while his heart quickened anxiously.

They had gone several blocks and reached a quiet road leading out of town before she spoke again.

"I think I must have come to the wailing-wall stage," she confessed. "You said I could talk to you — "

"Yes, my dear?" He waited, his eyes fastened to the road.

Mary never told things well, and sometimes he found it a bit hard to follow, and he knew that interruptions would be fatal. He pieced it together as best he could — how Ridge was now working day and night, and how his letters had changed until one almost wondered — how hard it had become to write her own letters now that she had omitted so long to mention the existence of Alec — and would it be wise to go and see Ridge again at Easter, without warning, and try to set things right, or should she wait to be asked this time — and would it be wrong to accept Alec's invitation to Washington and then not marry him after all — because it would be *interesting*, wouldn't it, to see Washington with a real live general as your host — but wouldn't Alec misunderstand, and wouldn't Ridge object — and hadn't she better just go home for the Easter holidays and let them all simply hang there till they dried out. . . .

Professor Bronson was silent for a full minute when she had finished. There was still another choice she didn't even know about, he was thinking. She could take refuge with him from all these uncertainties and conflicting claims, and have a quiet life, if that was what she really wanted, which he was inclined to doubt. But if he mentioned that new alternative now he would only place himself on the other side where all the questions were. What she wanted now was answers.

"I think," he said slowly, with an inward prayer for wisdom, "I think your Carolina boy has a right to know about the soldier."

"I think so too now, but I should have told him long ago if I was going to. So I thought perhaps if I went to see him — "

"There's the makings of a fine quarrel between you there," said Professor Bronson.

"Oh, Ridge and I would never quarrel!"

"How do you know?"

"That's right, I don't, really," she conceded, remembering his raw nerves on the last day, when she had mentioned her money.

"You say he told you to look round while you waited," Professor Bronson reminded her.

"And so he could hardly be jealous of Alec, could he, when I tell him?" She gave him a hopeful glance.

"But I think, the more you intend to marry him, the more you should do as he asked. You should make sure. You don't want to go into this thing with blinkers on, that's no kindness to him. I think he would want you to know exactly what you will be giving up for him — and I think it would be healthy for your own sake to make sure. There are bound to be times, later on, when things are a little out of tune, and you would find yourself wondering if you had chosen wrong, and if the soldier would have made you happier. But if first you go and see what your life with the soldier would be like, and *then* choose to live on the plantation — you haven't left any loopholes for regrets."

"But what about Alec? Is that fair to him?"

"You could make it fair. You must make it quite clear to him before you go to Washington that your visit is not in the nature of a promise."

It was rather an academic judgment, but neither Mary

nor Professor Bronson was experienced enough to realize that. He had done the best he could for her, and she had no better counsel available.

"It's going to be difficult," said Mary. "I have to write two letters. One to Ridge, about Alec. And one to Alec, to make it quite clear."

"And after you come back from Washington you will have the whole spring term to think it out," said Professor Bronson. "You can't marry either of them before June, anyway."

Less than three months, he thought wincingly. Less than three months, and I lose her. Unless by some miracle neither of them will do, after all. . . . And for her that would be no miracle, but only a tragedy. . . .

XIX

Alec read the rather frightened letter with a smile, and began to lay his plans. Most girls would not have been so explicit. Most girls would have allowed him to turn Washington inside out for them whether they had any intention of marrying him or not. Mary laid it on the line. She believed that she was in love with another man. For the other man's sake, she wanted to be sure. If it was still worth while to Alec like that, she would come.

During his lunch hour he went into a telegraph office and, still smiling, wrote on a yellow form: "Accept terms will proceed accordingly love Alec," it read.

Ridge read the rather frightened letter which revealed the existence of Alec with a queer, gone-in-the-middle sensation of having known it for some time. In any case it was not surprising. If it had not been Alec, it would have been somebody else, though Alec's rank and glamor came as an oddly fitting coincidence. Or was it only that?

Sitting alone in the lamplight at the end of the dining-room table at Avalon, with a spring rain falling outside and

[183]

a pile of dull deeds and mortgages awaiting his attention, a little groggy with overwork and abstinence and solitude, Ridge entertained involuntarily the more than passing idea that the General himself, dead a hundred and seventy years, could have returned, a daemon lover, to claim his own. And if this were so, had any mortal man a hope of altering the course of destiny? And even if it were just an eerie fancy, born of the shadows and his lonely fatigue, who would say that Alec, solvent and responsible and settled and sure, equipped to keep a girl like Mary safe and happy, with no waiting, no hoarding, no makeshifting about such daily amenities as a tight roof, an income, and bathrooms, was not meant to be? The only reason no one had fallen in love with her before was the unnaturally cloistered life she had lived. And if he was going to lose her, as he might very well do, Ridge preferred it to be now rather than later.

DEAR MARY [he wrote, at the end of the dining-room table, that night]:

Of course you must go to Washington. This is exactly what I meant when I said you might find something better if you looked. And if this proves to be it, you must not grieve. Only one thing I ask of you — don't try to hide it, don't ever lie to me, with some idea of letting me down easy. Because I shall know, and that will be worse.

I have felt in a way for some time that something like this was in the air. If I had not been so busy here I might have brought it into focus sooner. I want you to be happy even more than I want to marry you, can you understand that? And the last thing I want is for you to come back here out of a sense of obligation. Don't ever do that to me, will you. Take your time, use your head as well as your heart, and God bless you.

Love,

RIDGE

Then he went and got the whiskey bottle out of the sideboard.

X X

HE ROUSED UNWILLINGLY TO FIND MR. Conway standing over the bed. It was midday, and blinding sunlight was streaming into the room.

"Ridge, I want you at the office," Mr. Conway was saying, not for the first time. "Ridge, brace up — we've got a tough job on our hands at the office — "

"Yes, all right — all right — sorry — " He sat up and a shaft of pain ran through him, beginning back of the eyes. His tie was undone, but he had fallen asleep in his clothes — even his shoes. He swayed on the edge of the bed, his head in his hands, fighting his stomach, which threatened to disgrace him.

"My dear boy — " Mr. Conway sat down on the bed beside him, and put a hand on his shoulder. "You're in bad shape. I had no idea — "

"Ask Jeb for some coffee, will you?" said Ridge without moving, and heard Mr. Conway go to the top of the stairs and call, and heard Jeb's answering voice. When Mr. Conway returned to the room Ridge spoke again, still motionless. "I suppose you won't believe this is the first time. But it is."

"Of course I believe it if you say so," Mr. Conway replied quietly. "You've been asking too much of yourself for some time."

"It's not the work —" said Ridge, and bit off the rest of it too late.

"Trouble with your girl?" When he did not answer, Mr. Conway sighed, and his fingers gripped Ridge's arm in a sympathetic gesture immediately withdrawn. "The best of them let us down sometimes," he said. "Sometimes it's not as bad as it looks at first."

Jeb hurried in with a tray and two cups and a large pot of coffee. He set the tray down on the bedside table and poured for both of them, and at a glance from Mr. Conway held a cup under Ridge's nose.

"Coffee, Marse Ridge."

Ridge took the cup without the saucer and sat still where he was, sipping the strong, scalding brew while the mists cleared a little. Mr. Conway received his own cup from Jeb's hand and said tactfully, "I'll drink this downstairs — take your time."

As he left the room Jeb went to the bureau and began laying out a clean shirt and tie, socks and underwear.

"Be with you in a few minutes, sir," Ridge said, in a perfectly normal tone.

And he was, wearing a fresh suit, shaved, and with his wet hair carefully brushed. He had bought some new clothes and no longer looked mussed and seedy when he had not gone to sleep in them.

"Had breakfast?" he asked, looking in at the door of the parlor where Mr. Conway was.

"Had lunch," said Conway, and Ridge whistled.

"As bad as that?" he said. "I had a letter to write last night. Took me quite a while."

"Sure you want to send it now?"

"Quite sure. Care to come along to the dining-room and have a cup of coffee while I try to eat something? What did you think when I didn't show up this morning? Guessed right the first time, I bet!"

"It hasn't happened before," said Mr. Conway without complaint. "I was more surprised at that than I was this morning."

Ridge gave him his rueful smile as they sat down at the table with another pot of coffee between them, and Jeb brought in a plate of food.

"You said something about having something on our hands," Ridge suggested.

"There is going to be some trouble about Theodosia Sibley's will," said Mr. Conway.

"I thought she left everything to her sister Miranda."

"She did, in a will I drew for her some time ago. She apparently made another will last winter, not long before she died. And the new will leaves Miranda without a roof over her head."

"*What?* They were devoted to each other!"

[188]

"Exactly. Either this new will is a forgery, or there must have been undue influence."

"By whom?" Ridge asked blankly.

"By that fellow Watson and his wife who stayed there during the hunting season."

"She left the place to *them?*" Ridge was incredulous.

"That's what this new will says."

"Oh, it's crazy — it's impossible! They can't get away with that!"

"I want to contest this will, Ridge. There's something wrong somewhere."

"Have you seen the — what's their name? — Watsons?"

"Briefly. They're coming back to the office this afternoon with some lawyer they've engaged in Charleston. You'll have to help me with this, Ridge — I'll need you — "
He sagged a little against the table, and his cup clinked into the saucer as though it was suddenly too heavy to hold.

"Aren't you well, sir?"

"I'm not feeling very spry, Ridge. I'm afraid I'll have to lean on you a bit for a thing like this — "

Ridge looked at him anxiously. Mr. Conway always carried a little glass ampoule of amyl nitrite wrapped in a clean handkerchief in his breast pocket for his angina, and once during an attack which came on at the office Ridge had learned how to break the glass in the handkerchief and hold the fumes under Mr. Conway's nose. It was frightening to see, and one day it would kill him, but most of the time there was little evidence in his erect carriage and capacity for hard work that he had any necessity to spare himself.

"Perhaps it would be better not to take this on, sir — if it's going to be a nasty fight."

"What, go back on Miranda Sibley now? I wouldn't dream of such a thing! You and I between us can surely handle anything some Yankee schemer has cooked up on a pair of trusting old ninnies who would invite the devil himself to dine if he was a good shot and buttered them up a bit!"

"Well, anything I can do, of course, sir, but — "

"Now, never mind about last night, that's over and done with," said Mr. Conway, dismissing it with an impatient gesture. "Forget it. You were upset, and you took a few drinks. I've done the same myself. I've no doubts about you any more, Ridge, you're a born lawyer and it's time you carried your full share of responsibility at the office — and with full pay. Besides, having a good tough case like this one to deal with, you'll find that women take their proper place in your perspective — a little to the rear of center." He saw Ridge grin at his coffee cup doubtfully, and added, "I'll admit that's easier to say at my age than at yours, but you'll learn. What happened, anyway?"

"What you might expect."

"Somebody else?"

Ridge nodded.

"Has she called the whole thing off, then?"

"No. But you can't blame her if she does. I don't blame

her." He lighted a cigarette, but his hands were steady now. "About this tough case of Miss Miranda's," he said. "How do the Watsons come into it?"

"Chimneys was left to Theodosia by their father's will, because she was considerably older than Miranda, and was always supposed to have better sense," Mr. Conway explained. "Tom Sibley's will stipulated that Miranda should consider it her home as well, although at that time there was some possibility that one or both of the girls might marry. A few years ago Theodosia drew a will leaving the place to Miranda for her lifetime, and after her death, as there is no immediate family left, it was to go to some cousins in Charlotte on the distaff side. After that, Miranda says there was a lot of talk with the Watsons about not letting the place run down — putting money into it to keep it in repair, caring for it as they had not been able to do for years themselves, and as the Charlotte cousins might neglect to do, as they have never shown any interest in it. That line of talk by the Watsons would have been a strong influence on both the girls, as they always took great pride in the house. They undoubtedly thought it would be preserved, in the Watsons' hands. So Theodosia drew yet another will, which is the one we're up against now.

"Miss Miranda acquiesced in the new will, then?"

"She knew about it, which was more than I did. The first I heard of it was after Theodosia died when Miranda gave me the Watson's address in New York and said there was a new will — just as I was about to proceed with the old one in the belief that it was the only one which existed. Theodosia was probably scared to tell me what she had done. I wrote the Watsons at once, and they have arrived post-haste with their document. As Miranda understood it at the time, and as Theodosia doubtless intended it, Miranda still had the right to live in the house for the rest of her life, at which time the property was to pass wholly into the possession of Mr. and Mrs. Watson. However, in the will they have presented for probate there is no mention of Miranda. They are given the property outright, so that they could put her out at once if they chose to do so, and they have served notice on her to that effect. They want full possession immediately on settlement of the estate. There is no doubt about Theodosia's signature. But I am convinced that either she didn't know the will had been changed to eliminate Miranda or she was somehow persuaded that it didn't matter."

"Miss Theodosia wasn't very bright, towards the last," Ridge said. "It would have been fairly easy to get her to sign something without her understanding quite what it was she was putting her name to. Who witnessed it?"

"Friends of Mr. and Mrs. Watson, who just happened to be there at the time — like the lawyer, allegedly from New Jersey, who drew it while they were still in the house. He was another friend of the Watsons whose presence was opportune."

"And who is the executor?"

"Mr. Watson himself is named executor of the new will.

I was executor of the old one," said Mr. Conway with some asperity.

"The Watsons seem to have thought of everything." Ridge got up and walked around the table, smoking, and then sat down again, and poured another cup of coffee. "But it doesn't smell right," he said then. "In the first place, Miss Theodosia didn't *like* the guests she took into her house for the hunting. That is, she put up with them, as a necessary evil. They were never allowed to feel that they were only there on sufferance and because she needed the money, that wouldn't have fitted in with her ideas of hospitality. But she was not the sort of person to get fond of people she always regarded as interlopers — not fond enough to leave them the place unconditionally — certainly not at the expense of Miss Miranda's expectations. What I'm getting at is, she wouldn't have been carried away by these Watsons on the strength of a few promises by them."

"I wouldn't think so," said Mr. Conway wearily.

"We're in this, are we?" Ridge asked, point-blank. "We're going to try to break this will?"

"We are."

"What are they like — the Watsons?"

"Come and see for yourself. Miranda says they were pleasant, friendly people in the house — always made a great fuss of the place — last winter, when the will was drawn, was their third visit, so they must have been working on it for some time."

"That's another thing that puzzles me," said Ridge. "If

they have the kind of money to go and stay there for the hunting every year, surely they could have bought and sold the Sibley girls twice over. Why go to all the trouble and risk of tampering with a will?"

"Remains to be seen," said Mr. Conway. "They're due back at the office at four o'clock this afternoon, with their lawyer."

Ridge rose.

"Let's go," he said.

He picked up the letter he had written to Mary, and posted it on his way to the office.

XXI

M R. AND MRS. WATSON ARRIVED AT MR.
Conway's office promptly at four, with an unexceptional
lawyer engaged in Charleston by them that day. The
lawyer who had drawn the will, they explained, was an
elderly man and had fallen ill during a visit to his daughter
in California, and was not now available to appear on their
behalf. But the married couple named Smith who had signed
the will as witnesses were at present in Charleston and
could be called upon if necessary.

The Watsons were a quietly dressed, affluent-looking
pair, who maintained with inflexible pleasantness that they
needed the space occupied by Miss Miranda in the house,
and could not recall any sort of understanding with her
late sister that she was to retain any rights whatever in the
estate. They were very sorry in a perfunctory way, but
they had assumed that she was otherwise provided for, and
it was really no affair of theirs where she spent the rest of
her life — which they implied wouldn't be long, anyway,
and therefore wasn't very important. The cool callousness

of them was dumfounding, and the interview was brief, amounting to a declaration of war on both sides.

When they had gone, Mr. Conway and Ridge sat down to plan their case.

Miss Miranda, of course, remained in possession at Chimneys. The Watsons went into residence at the one small hotel in town where Mary had stayed. They did not mingle much, partly because their presence was not welcome to those in the community who knew about the will, as local sentiment was on Miss Miranda's side. They usually spent the day in Charleston, where their witnesses, Mr. and Mrs. Smith, seemed to have a host of acquaintances, if not in the best circles. Or they all went to a beach club nearly two hours drive away, where they had established relations with a rather spendthrift crew of friends — returning each evening, or in the small hours, as though to maintain squatters' rights on the scene. Or was it, Ridge began to wonder, because the living was cheaper that way.

Ridge wanted time, more than anything else — time to observe the Watsons and solve their odd behavior. He had often lunched at the hotel, instead of going home, and now he took to dropping in more frequently, in the vague hope of picking up some information which might contribute to the mystery of why people with the kind of money the Watsons appeared to have should prefer to live so economically when not in the midst of their well-heeled associates. There was some subterranean reason, he felt sure, for their continued presence in surroundings to which they were obviously quite indifferent except as a base of operations. Either the Watsons were hiding out, he decided — and from whom — or else they were hard up. And if they were hard up, there was a motive, perhaps, for trying to swindle Miss Theodosia out of her house. Though why Chimneys was worth their while, even then, was still a mystery to him. If they were unable to pay cash for it, unable anyway to acquire it honestly until after Miss Miranda's death, they might have tried some form of short cut to its possession. Why? How did they happen to come to Chimneys in the beginning? And why did they keep coming back?

On an afternoon in March, when Ridge stopped in the lobby to buy a paper and some cigarettes and have what he called a sniff round, the desk clerk caught his eye.

"Ridge — just in case you're interested, there is a Mr. Wilkins here, asking for the Watsons."

"Where?"

"In the Coffee Shop, now."

"Did he register?"

"No. Asked about rooms, said tell them he was here, and went in to get a cup of tea, he said."

"Luggage?"

"Still in his car, I suppose. They won't be back till late, probably, but I didn't say that."

"Good for you. What's he like?"

"Young — respectable — having his tea and reading his paper at the fourth wall table from this end."

"Thanks. And when they come — forget to tell them about him."

Ridge entered the Coffee Shop, glanced round casually, and sat down at the third table, on the bench which ran along the wall, and ordered coffee. Except for a couple of travelling salesmen, having a belated lunch or an early dinner, the place was deserted. He glanced once or twice at the man with the newspaper sitting next him on the bench, and was ignored. Finally he said conversationally, "Aren't you Aston Carpenter?"

"No," said the stranger, surprised but courteous. "My name is Wilkins."

"Oh, sorry. Mine's — Fletcher. I could have sworn you were with my outfit in the Pacific, and I couldn't but wonder what brought you here."

"I paint, as a matter of fact," said Mr. Wilkins rather self-consciously. "I've been up at the Beach on a job."

"That's interesting. I'm a writer, myself. Supposed to be."

"Books?" Mr. Wilkins showed a friendly interest.

"A book. You wouldn't have heard of it. What do you paint — seascapes?"

"Murals, at the moment." Young Mr. Wilkins gave him a humorous, confidential look. "On bathrooms, this was! This old lady at the Beach with pots of money wanted a lot of fish and seaweed on her bathroom walls and couldn't find any wall paper to suit her — so I painted them on. As a matter of fact, I made quite a nice job of it!"

"An old house?" Ridge asked idly, as his coffee arrived. "Or one of those modern palaces?"

"This one was new, but I adore old houses. That's partly why I came here, I'm hoping to see some of the old plantations and get some ideas."

"I've got one of those myself," Ridge threw out. "You can see mine, if you like."

"Oh, you have? That's marvellous. Did you ever hear of a house called Chimneys somewhere around here?"

"Vaguely," said Ridge. "Up north of town, isn't it? Couple of old ladies."

"One of them died recently," said Mr. Wilkins. "Some friends of mine inherited the house. Well, not friends, exactly, they're just people I know," he amended, as though not wishing to claim acquaintance with the great. "They're going to remodel it for some sort of club, I believe, and put in a half-dozen more bathrooms and redecorate — as a matter of fact, I'm hoping to get the job."

"Well, here's luck," said Ridge, raising his coffee cup as though it were a cocktail, and contriving not to point like a bird-dog as Mr. Wilkins went on spilling the beans. It was the first indication from anybody of the use the Watsons intended to make of the house. "Sounds as though there would probably be plenty of money involved," he suggested.

"Well, no, as a matter of fact, I'm not at all sure there is," said Mr. Wilkins confidentially. "Between you and me, I think it's some kind of deal, myself, to get the backing.

They'll probably turn it into one of those plush hideouts for the gambling crowd. There's a new highway going through quite near it, you probably know all about that if you live around here."

"Oh, yes," said Ridge, purposely unconcerned, though the new highway was already causing some extra work at Mr. Conway's office. "I see the connection. You think they're probably stooges for somebody who puts up the capital?"

"Or else they're taking a long shot themselves on a shoe-string. I'd certainly want some kind of guarantee before I put in much time there. And then there's another thing, there seems to be some trouble about the will. Some lawyer here says it's a fake, or something. Though I don't really see how there can be any doubt about that. I was there when they all signed it. It's a lovely old house, that was what really got me interested in these old plantations. In restoring them, you know. I'd much rather do that kind of work than these so-called modern improvements, but you have to take whatever comes along in my business."

Ridge set down his cup gently.

"I'm on my way home now," he said. "Would you like to come out and see my place? It's not far from town — and quite unrestored."

"Oh, I'd love to! My car is just outside, and the Watsons haven't come back yet."

"Mine is still at the garage and may not be ready to drive," said Ridge. "I was killing time here, waiting for it.

If you'd care to run us out and then bring me back with you, I could pick it up then."

"Why, certainly, I'd be glad to!"

They paid their bills, and Mr. Wilkins left the Coffee Shop at Ridge's side, a lamb to the slaughter.

In the midst of his guest's preliminary exclamations of pleasure over Avalon, Ridge guided him into Alice's sitting-room and sent Jeb for sherry, which appeared at once with fragile, bell-shaped glasses on a silver tray.

"Mr. Wilkins," said Ridge rather abruptly, interrupting a rhapsody over Alice's needlepoint chairs, "I'm afraid I must apologize for bringing you here under false pretences. My name is Creston, and I am Miss Miranda's lawyer in the will case."

Mr. Wilkins looked upset, and was speechless.

"Forgive all this hocus-pocus," said Ridge, "but at first I couldn't be sure that you weren't here at the Watson's request."

"Oh, no, as a matter of fact they didn't even know I was coming, they — "

"And then I wanted to get you out of the hotel before they came in," said Ridge.

"Oh, dear, have I said something?" Mr. Wilkins was definitely alarmed.

"You've said something very interesting. You were there when the will was signed."

"Well, yes, but — "

"You seem, if I may say so, a very regular sort of a guy,

[201]

Mr. Wilkins. Have you any idea what is going on about that will?"

"Why, no, I — Going *on?*" repeated Mr. Wilkins with apprehension.

"You saw Miss Miranda when you were staying at the house, didn't you? What did you think of her?"

"Why, she was an absolute darling! They were both wonderful to me. As a matter of fact, I fell in love with them both!"

"Then when I say that if this will stands it will rob her of her home and leave her stranded for the rest of her life with nowhere to go and nothing to live on, you might be willing to answer a few questions?"

"That dear old lady? I never *dreamed*, I thought — " Mr. Wilkins was visibly ruffled and incredulous. "Well, as you say, what *is* going on?" he demanded indignantly. "I thought everything was all aboveboard at the time. That is, everything was all very friendly, and the sister certainly made no objection to the will when it was signed."

"Were you in the room, at the actual signing?"

"Why, yes, I was, as a matter of fact."

"May I ask if Mr. and Mrs. Watson are not close friends of yours, how you happened to be there with them?"

"Well, it was sort of accidental, I was at a place near Southern Pines doing a cocktail bar for one of the horsey crowd," Mr. Wilkins explained. "They wanted horses' heads on everything in sight, it really was — well, never mind about that. And these people, the Watsons, showed up there, and were on their way down here, and we got talking about Southern architecture — you know how it is — and they told about this marvellous place run by these two old ladies where you lived practically like one of the family — at a price, of course! Well, I just thought I'd like to see it, and so when they said Come along, I did — just like that! As a matter of fact, I was sort of drifting, you know the way you do, and the cocktail bar was finished, and I'd been paid off, and I thought it sounded like fun. And then when it came up that night about the will, I didn't think anything about it one way or the other — if I'd had any *idea* — but it was all very sort of casual, I was just sitting there reading a book — "

"Would it in your opinion have been possible for Miss Theodosia to have signed a document which had been sub- stituted for the one she meant to sign?"

Mr. Wilkins regarded him with large, shocked eyes.

"Oh, dear — was that what they did?"

"I want to know if they could have done it," said Ridge. "You can keep me if you will. Who else was present? What were the circumstances?"

"Well, there was this other couple who were travelling with the Watsons — named Smith, believe it or not! And there was the lawyer who had drawn up the will, he was already in the house when we got there. That made five of them, and me, and the two Miss Sibleys."

"Did Miss Theodosia seem — competent?"

"Oh, yes." Mr. Wilkins gave him an amused look.

"Vague, you know — and fluttery, and sweet — but I'd say all there."

"What was the first you heard about a will?"

"Why, it was after dinner one night. We were all sitting round relaxing, having a liqueur with coffee, and I had picked up this book, and somebody said something about the Smiths leaving the next day, and then somebody, I think it was Mr. Watson, said they might as well finish up the business part of the visit that evening, while they had the witnesses, and the lawyer — I've forgotten his name but I'd know it if I heard it again — went and got his brief-case and took out some papers and told them where to sign, and that was that!"

"Now — just a minute, this is important. You say he took papers out of a brief-case in your presence which were signed then and there. But didn't Miss Theodosia before she signed read the will herself, page by page?"

"No — she couldn't have, it only took a few minutes for the whole thing. I remember getting up myself to hunt for her spectacles and she just put them on and wrote her name. Oh, she initialled each page, you know, the way you have to — but she just marked it where they told her to, without stopping to read it."

Ridge was silent so long that Mr. Wilkins grew uneasy.

"Does that prove anything?" he asked, draining his glass nervously.

"It seems to prove that there could have been a substitution," said Ridge, preoccupied. "Mr. Wilkins — would you be willing to appear as a witness in this case for Miss Miranda?"

"Well, I — if you think it would help her, I'd be glad to. The Watsons are nothing to me."

"You'll lose your job, you know. That is, if we win they won't be turning the place into a club and there won't be any work for you."

Mr. Wilkins waved a hand.

"So what?" he said. "I didn't have the job anyway, as a matter of fact. When I heard at the Beach that they were here, I just thought I'd pop down and see if they'd made any arrangements for redecorating."

"I'd like you to stay out of sight till we're ready. Would you mind passing a week or so here as my guest in the meantime?"

"I'd love it," said Mr. Wilkins easily, with a glance round at the exquisite little sitting-room. "All these books to browse in — and the garden — but I left a message for the Watsons at the hotel — "

"I cancelled it," said Ridge. "I hope you don't mind."

"No, I never did anything like this before, it's very exciting," said Mr. Wilkins. "Will I have to get up in the witness chair and tell all I know?"

Ridge grinned. Mr. Wilkins was a strangely disarming, rather pathetic young man in his drifting, catch-as-catch-can existence, and the Watsons had made their one mistake in treating him as negligible.

"We'll see you through all that," Ridge promised, and

went to tell Jeb there would be company for dinner.

There was a telephone now at Avalon, and Ridge arranged to have his car brought out from where he had left it in front of the office — the garage story was all part of the hocus-pocus — and in a guarded call to Mr. Conway invited him to drive over to dinner that evening and discuss an urgent new development.

He had clean forgotten, when he returned to Mr. Wilkins in the parlor, that Mary's Easter vacation had begun.

XXII

ALEC'S UNIFORMED DRIVER WAS WAITING
at the airport when Mary and Sally arrived on an afternoon
which was already spring in Washington. They followed
him to the big blue Cadillac, which wafted them past the
impressive Pentagon building with its faintly Babylonian
look, and across the bridge to a quiet Georgetown street.
Alec's charming red brick house had a fresh write trim and
small-paned windows, and stood in a tiny garden.

A smiling colored houseman opened the door to them,
a soft-voiced colored maid was waiting upstairs to unpack
for them, and they went down to tea in a long drawing-
room furnished in pure Williamsburg style, with a wood
fire burning. For Sally, of course, the friendly servants, the
casual luxury, the perfection of polish and texture and do-
mestic temperature were no novelty. She called the servants by name, she asked for *more* cinnamon toast and it
was taken by all concerned as a compliment if not a favor
conferred on the kitchen, she sprawled gracefully on the
down cushions of the fireside sofa, her sharp high heels
dug into the deep pile of the rug — she was the master's

only sister, she belonged here, always welcome and lovingly cherished. But Mary too, as the master's guest, was enveloped in the cordial concern and cheerful cosseting of his household. And while she was accustomed to comfort and tidiness and good food at home, this was wealth, and the special, intangible smoothness of life among people to whom the mere mechanics of existence are taken entirely for granted — doors open, food arrives and vanishes, fires are lighted, beds are turned down, there is always someone to answer a bell — and here in Georgetown all this was evident without any of the strangeness and lurking formality of the Boston week-end. Mary was conscious from the beginning of an odd sense of usualness and familiarity in Alec's house, almost as though she had been there before, as though it awaited her, as though, however gently, it laid hold of her. Which she at once told herself in alarm Wouldn't Do.

Presently, while they still sat idly, a little drowsy with the fire, making effortless female conversation, the houseman, whose name was Vernon, came and spirited away the tea things and switched on a shaded lamp. Sally struggled with a ladylike yawn and reached for another cigarette, and somewhere in the house a clock struck softly.

"Why don't you smoke one?" said Sally. "It helps to pass the time. I could do with a drink, but we'll wait till Alec comes if he's not too long."

Mary reached out and took a cigarette from the box on the table between them, and lighted it.

"I've tried smoking," she said. "But I never get used to the way the taste of tobacco stays on my fingers and tongue."

"A fan is more your style," Sally commented. "That's what it really amounts to, you know. The modern woman hasn't got a fan to fool with, and not knowing what to do with her hands she smokes cigarettes."

"I never thought of it like that," said Mary, much struck.

A door closed gently, Vernon passed through the hall, and Alec was there.

"Heigh-ho," he said as he entered, bringing with him a masculine aura of pipe-smoke and outdoors. "Here you are, and a very pleasant sight, I must say, at the end of a hard day." He gave Sally a resounding brotherly kiss and then as though it was quite the natural thing to do he kissed Mary lightly, easily, on the cheek, leaning across the back of the sofa where she sat. "Had your tea? All comfy?" He caught hold of Mary's hand and removed the cigarette from her fingers, setting it casually between his own lips. "Doesn't suit you to smoke," he said parenthetically. "Don't ever do it."

"Everything is beautiful," Mary assured him, smiling. "Especially the cinnamon toast!"

"I suppose you made horrible schoolgirl pigs of yourselves," he remarked with satisfaction. "It's just as well dinner will be late."

"Oh, now, Alec, not one of *those!*" wailed Sally.

"Embassies and all," he said cheerfully. "Got to do it

once in a while, you know, and always make the most of having a beautiful hostess here."

"Blarney," said Sally. "You'll scare Mary out of a year's growth to begin with."

"She might as well know the worst, don't you think?"

"There's plenty of time for that!"

"Tomorrow night will be nice and easy, we dine with the Mackenzies. And the next night I've got seats for some show or other, anyway it's cheerful. I've arranged for you to have the Cadillac while you're here, with Pringle to drive it — unless of course you'd rather take the small car and drive yourself."

"Thanks very much, I think it would be rather nice to just sit back and be driven, I'll leave it to Pringle."

"Good. Collingwood will be open, you'll want to lunch there one day, and see the Lee House and so on. There are some notes and messages and things on your dressing-table from people who are dying to be good to you."

"I saw. But I didn't *look*," said Sally, and stretched like a cosy cat. "I'm relaxing, darling. I work hard too."

"Yes, I'm sure you do. But get at the messages, won't you, when you've had a drink and a bath," he added inflexibly.

"O.K., General!" said Sally, with a rude salute, and Mary thought, The iron hand — love, honor, and *obey*. . . .

Vernon arrived on cue with a large tray of bottles, glasses, and ice, which he arranged with care on a side table, and Mary felt again that unreal sensation she had experienced more than once during the Boston visit — that she was taking an unrehearsed part in a smart drawing-room comedy where everyone else knew their lines and she had come on as some sort of understudy without the faintest idea of what was going to happen next or what the author intended her to do.

"Sherry for Mary," Alec brought her the frail stemmed glass, without asking what she would like, and returned to the tray. "Martini for Sally, Bourbon for Alec. Very simple tastes we have, really. Takes very little to make us happy." Ice and glass tinkled briefly, efficiently, under his hands, and he returned to the fire with two more glasses. "There you are, Sally, my little drunkard. Mary, darling — " He lifted his glass to her — "thank you for coming."

They sipped, in an intimate, comfortable pause, and Alec sat down on the sofa beside Sally, facing Mary across the fire. "Now, I'll just brief you on who is coming tonight," he said, and did so, at some length. Nine guests and themselves. A seating plan was produced, while Mary sat silent and uneasy, reflecting that this charming little house might about as well be Buckingham Palace with all this discussion of rank, embassies, and air force, and names heard on the radio.

"You're depressing Mary," said Sally finally. "Don't be so darned executive, Alec. It's that horrible Pentagon dust settling on you already."

"I shouldn't wonder," he agreed cheerfully. "Well, anyway — that's the works. Have another?"

"Not now, thanks. I'm going up and take a bath and un-kink before I start dressing."

Mary rose too, and started to follow Sally toward the door, when Alec caught her hand and said, "She's only being tactful, don't you see? Sit down a minute, there's no rush."

Sally looked back at them, laughing, and continued into the hall and up the staircase.

"It's a wonderful house, Alec, I never saw anything like it," Mary said a little too quickly, recovering her hand.

"Come and see the rest of it."

She followed him into the hall and around the ground floor rooms — dining-room full of dark mahogany and heavy polished silver, small drawing-room done in sage green and yellow, panelled library full of leather upholstery and a man-sized desk — all so finished and complete and permanent, with nothing left to be desired.

"But it seems so — settled," Mary said, puzzled and fascinated. "Did you find it like this, or — surely you haven't just moved in."

"Oh, it's been here for years," Alec said easily. "Just as you see it. Since before the war, you know. It was closed up, of course, all the time I was in Germany."

"I see," said Mary faintly. For years, just as she saw it. Then his wife must have lived here. It was her taste, these were her things. And when she left it for the divorce, it was closed up. Silly to feel disappointment or embarrassment. Silly to feel that it mattered. Surely she had not supposed that the house had been put together just for herself. She had not supposed anything at all, till now. Therefore she had not expected it to be his wife's house. No personal trace of a woman's presence in it now remained. No photographs, no — well, naturally, no belongings. But — it had been another woman's house. She felt a faint, fastidious recoil.

"That doesn't mean you can't do anything you like with it, if you decide to stay," Alec said, as though reading her thoughts, and at her startled upward glance he laughed indulgently, and laid a possessive arm around her, holding her against his side. "Am I forbidden to mention that?" he asked. "Why do you always look so frightened? Almost as though you thought I'd take advantage of you now, in my own house! I'm much too old a campaigner to make a tactical error like that!" Still he held her, looking down into her face. "Now what? Don't you like being thought of as a complicated maneuver to be won?"

"But — I told you before I came — " she began unhappily.

"All right. You told me. But no harm in trying, is there?"

And just as she thought with panic that he was going to kiss her, he took his arm away and opened the library door for her to precede him into the hall again. Alec was indeed a great tactician.

"Be beautiful tonight," he said softly. "Not that you can help it."

"You mean you want me to make an Impression?" she suggested, smiling, and he laughed again.

"You will," he promised. "Now, run along to Sally, I've got my home-work to do."

He returned to the study, closing the door behind him, and Mary thoughtfully mounted the stairs. Her best dress, he meant. The rose-colored cloud Sally had bullied her into buying. Well, she might as well get the good of it, it was unsuitable for anything else but this visit.

The evening was brilliant with oversize personalities, dress clothes, French-English conversation — the Embassy counselor and his jewelled wife — stiff British military, a famous news commentator inclined to sardonic brevity, and good old stand-by Mack, whom Mary welcomed with excessive relief, though she was not allowed the indulgence of sitting by him. Dazzled, stimulated, a little awed, a little out of her depth, Mary drank champagne and responded with deceptive composure to the amused sallies of the French counselor and the rather ponderous gallantry of the handsome Briton. Both of them patronized her just a little, but she was meekly aware that she deserved no better, and envied Sally's brittle assurance of manner. Sometimes she caught Alec's glance briefly, and knew that he kept track of her, and wondered if she was being a disappointment to him. I could never live like this, she thought with a kind of satisfaction, as though something had been settled by this first demonstration. It's quite beyond me, maybe he'll see that now. *They* know it's beyond me. They wonder why I'm here.

Perhaps it was the champagne. But when, several courses

[214]

later, everyone rose from the table, she had made the Frenchman laugh heartily, and the Briton was anything but supercilious. In the drawing-room, when the men returned to it, a bridge-table materialized — but only one, so there were also conversation groups, and Mack gravitated to Mary's side with a certain effect of old times, and Alec was never far away. His eyes were kind, and he seemed to feel that she was doing well. She did not realize that she had lifted to him the disciplined, anxious look of a child at a new school.

When the last guest had departed, Sally's hostess smile fell from her face with something like a thud and she led the way back to the fireside sofa and dropped there, kicking off her silver slippers with abandon and reaching for a cigarette. The room was heavy with cigarette smoke, the ashtrays were messy, empty glasses stood about, the fire had burned low.

"Whew!" said Sally. "Really, I suppose it's a lot *quieter* than the Battle of the Bulge, but you can overdo it a bit!"

"You call *tonight* dull!" Alec snorted, clinking ice into a glass at the drink tray. "You ought to see some of the others! Have a nightcap, anybody?"

"No, thanks. It wasn't dull, exactly, it was just *taxing*. Why is it so hard to talk to them?"

Alec returned to the fireside with a mild Bourbon for himself and a glass of freshly opened tonic water which he handed to Mary as he sat down beside her. She noticed that, like taking the cigarette out of her fingers earlier in the day, he now gave her what he thought she should have, without consulting her. It was at once a protective and subtly domineering procedure which roused in her a perverse inward query as to whether it really was what she wanted. The commanding officer. Orders. Ridge would have inquired first. And if she had said goat's milk, he would have tried to find her some before he so much as sat down. . . . She saw herself meekly accepting the glass from Alec's hand with a docile smile. Life with Alec would require very little initiative. Choices, however small, would all be made for one — until, perhaps, one's own power of decision atrophied and dropped off?

Sipping her tonic water, which she was now quite sure she didn't care for, Mary wondered what would have happened if she had announced firmly that she would like some gin in it. Meanwhile the comfortable family post mortem rambled on around her.

"I didn't notice," Alec was saying without criticism, "that you had trouble talking."

"Oh, well, one always thinks of *something*," said Sally without animus. "But the *effort!* I suppose living here all the time would make a difference. Our little chickie, there, was doing all right with the French Embassy!"

"Chickie does all right, period," said Alec, glancing affectionately at their guest.

"It was uphill all the way," Mary remarked, sipping her tonic water, and they laughed as though she had said something very funny indeed.

Sally finished her cigarette and put out the stub, picked up her slippers in her hand, and stood up in her stocking feet.

"This isn't tact, or what do you call it," she said. "I'm simply falling asleep. And I will *not* see you at breakfast. Good-night, all."

And she padded away up the stairs, carrying her slippers, leaving two half-emptied glasses and a silence behind her in the drawing-room.

Mary set down her glass and looked at the doorway doubtfully, wishing that Sally had left any opening for her own escape.

"In a minute, don't rush off," Alec said easily, reading her mind as usual. His own glass stood on the little table at his elbow, a newly lighted cigarette was in his fingers. "Was it too bad tonight, or do you think you could get used to it?"

"I felt sort of like a country cousin."

"They liked that." He turned to her, sliding one arm along the back of the sofa. "So do I. That's a wonderful dress. You look like an apple-blossom."

"What a lovely compliment!" Mary smiled with artless pleasure, and realized that he had her blockaded in the corner of the sofa, that he could kiss her unless she fought him, and that he was going to.

Perhaps it was the champagne, but she didn't resist as he bent over her. It was a deliberate kiss, gentle and possessive, and while she did not exactly respond, the impulse to clout him was not there. Belatedly, it seemed to her that he might misunderstand.

"Oh, Alec, I'm sorry, I – didn't – "

"That's what *I'm* supposed to be saying!" he observed with considerable amusement. " 'I didn't mean to presume on your being here as my guest,' or some such remark. It wasn't in the bond, I know that. Something just came over me, shall we say."

"I shouldn't have let you, I – "

"It would have been pretty hard to stop me." He rose with a sort of sigh. "No harm done. But whether I win this game or not, I hope that Carolina business is safely over and done with."

Mary stared at him in surprise and alarm.

"Oh, no!" she cried hastily. "That's why – I mean, I thought I made it quite clear – "

"You did." His smile was a little grim, and he made no move towards her as she stood up as though for flight. "But I still think that sort of life is not for you. You're not the strong, silent, motherly type, if I may say so. You want cherishing – with the things that money can buy. Pretty clothes, and a chance to show them – champagne – break-fast in bed – your own checkbook – and a sober, industrious, idolatrous husband – like me, for instance. Which reminds me, you've had rather a long day, and I still have some desk-work to do before I can turn in."

"I had no idea generals were such slaves to duty," she said, rallying.

"Some of us work at it," he admitted carelessly. "Breakfast will come to your room, in the morning. Just ring when you want it. Good-night, my dear."

He looked suddenly tired, she thought, a trifle hag-ridden, and — solitary. In a warm rush of sympathy, she wished she could help. A man like Alec, carrying heavy responsibility gallantly, ought to have *somebody*. . . .

"Good-night, Alec," she said gently, and went away, up the stairs, and heard the door of the library close behind him.

Well, I can't look after them both, she thought wearily, preparing for bed. And Alec has heaps of chances. There are a lot of people better qualified than I am for this sort of thing. You look like an apple-blossom, he had said. The loveliest compliment she had ever had. And then he went on to prescribe the sort of life *he* thought best for her — not waiting to hear what she might want instead. The things that money could buy sounded very alluring. But what about Avalon in its lost beauty, and Ridge with his lost years? What about the small miracle it would be to see Ridge take his rightful place in his own world, and Avalon bloom again under her hands to the burnished perfection of Chimneys? That was something to *do*, something to accomplish, not just the decorative idleness which was apparently all Alec thought she was good for. She dwelt again on his kiss, which had not at all repelled her, but neither had it made her see stars, as Ridge's did. That's funny, she thought, getting into bed. According to all the rules, I ought to have reacted more. People who get kissed by the wrong man are supposed to feel outraged and virtuous, but I didn't, not a bit. Perhaps because Alec is so very kind and good . . . Perhaps if it wasn't for Ridge. . . . What's the matter with me, she wondered, putting out the light. Haven't I got any morals? Don't I know my own mind? Can just *anybody* kiss me? She thought of Mack, and grinned in the dark. Oh, well, Mack. You couldn't keep your face straight with him. But it was illuminating, to learn from Alec that one was only human, after all. Whatever that meant. And of course tonight it didn't mean. . . . And of course it mustn't happen again. . . . But there were how many days still to go. . . .

XXIII

IT BECAME APPARENT THAT FIRST EVENING
at Fleetwood that with Mr. Wilkins up their sleeves they
were definitely making progress, but Mr. Conway was still
not satisfied. There was a missing link, he said. Miss
Theodosia appeared to have signed a will without reading
it. But there must have been a will which she had read and
approved at some previous conference with the Watsons'
lawyer.

Miss Miranda had seen such a will, she was quite sure.
And Miss Theodosia was not so gaga that she would not at
some point in the proceedings have had to be shown the
clause which protected her sister. If such a will, in Miss
Miranda's favor, had once existed, what had become of it,
Mr. Conway wanted to know, and who had made the ex-
change, and maneuvered Miss Theodosia into signing the
substituted one? Either the Watsons or their unavailable
lawyer, who if he had been a party to any such intent was
obviously no lawyer at all — which would probably account for his invisibility now. Mr. Conway wanted to
know more about the first will — when it was shown to

Miss Miranda and Miss Theodosia for their approval, when it was last seen by them, and who else might have seen it and could swear to its existence and to her intention.

The next morning Ridge left Mr. Wilkins browsing among the books in Alice's room and drove out to Chimneys. Miss Miranda was glad to see him, and offered him cake and Madeira wine. He saw at once that the shock of her sister's death and the subsequent disturbance about the will was aging her noticeably — she was preoccupied, unhappy, and she didn't always follow what was said to her. He began patiently to lead her memory back into the days just preceding the signing of the will on the evening Mr. Wilkins had described.

"Now, think carefully, because you can help us very much," he said gently, careful not to hurry or confuse her, building up her own self-confidence and sense of importance. "When did you first see the new will, which mentioned the Watsons?"

"It was the day after they came back last November, and Mr. Granger was here," she said quite positively. "Mr. Granger was their lawyer."

"Had Mr. Granger ever been here before?"

"No, that was his first visit."

"Why did he come?"

"I think they must have asked him to. Yes, I'm sure he was introduced to us by them. Because I thought at the time it was odd how little he seemed to care for the shooting."

"Yes, I see," said Ridge encouragingly. "Did he have

a copy of the will prepared before they arrived?"

"Oh, no, I don't think so. How would he have known?"

"Then did they all work it out together after the Watsons got here?"

"Well, we had talked about it the year before. And then it came up again that first evening, when they said how nice it was to be back, and what would become of Chimneys after both Theodosia and I were gone — and how they could take good care of it if they had it, because they had money to spend on it — and Theodosia hadn't been feeling very well, and I think perhaps she had a *premonition*. Because she decided that very night to leave it to them after me, instead of to that cousin in Charlotte who has never even bothered to come and see us — "

"And did she think of that herself, or was it suggested to her by the Watsons?"

Miss Miranda looked puzzled and confused.

"I don't remember. It *seemed* as though it came to Theodosia first — but since then sometimes I've wondered — "

"But you think the will was drawn up right here in the house, after that conversation?"

"It *seemed* that way — now, how was it, they said something about Mr. Granger having just done the same thing for somebody else, I forget where, and he said wills were quite simple, really, and if we liked he would make a — a draft, or something. He said he had noticed a typewriter in Mr. Smith's luggage — and if he could borrow that he could turn out a will in no time."

[223]

"He borrowed Mr. Smith's typewriter," said Ridge.

"Yes, he tapped away up in his bedroom for a while, and pretty soon he came down with the will in his hand."

"But you didn't see him actually write it."

"N-no, I don't think anybody did."

"Did you read it yourself? What he brought down in his hand."

"Oh, yes, I'm perfectly certain I saw the part where it said I had the house — " Miss Miranda's eyes overflowed and she got out her handkerchief. " — had the right to live in the house — till I died — " She was crying.

"Now, you mustn't do that, we won't worry yet, everything is going very nicely," said Ridge. "Now, you really must brace up because I need your help, you know. There are just one or two more things I would like to know, and you can't think straight if you go on crying — there — it's a good thing you aren't the kind to break down, or we'd never get anywhere. Now, tell me this — do you think anyone else saw the will while it was being discussed?"

"I — don't remember anybody — "

"Did either of you ask anyone's advice, or tell anybody about changing over to the Watsons?"

"Well, no, I don't think so — " But there seemed to be a slight cloud, a hazy recollection which eluded her.

"Think, now," Ridge encouraged her quietly. "Would she have written to anyone, such as the cousin in Charlotte, and mentioned the change?"

"No, I'm sure she didn't do that, because I remember her

saying to Letty Dunham that it would serve him right and he could find it out when the will was read — if he cared, which she doubted!"

"She said that to Mrs. Dunham," Ridge repeated cautiously, hoping to trap this glimmer of light without scaring it away. "Then Mrs. Dunham must have been here. When was that, do you think?"

Miss Miranda considered.

"She came to borrow something — or return something — I forget — anyway, Theodosia had the will right in her hand, and when Letty heard about the Watsons she said — " Miss Miranda looked worried and uncertain. "Well, they had quite a tiff. Letty spoke right out and said she didn't think Theodosia ought to leave it to any Yankees, no matter what."

"But didn't Mrs. Dunham know that you came first?" Ridge insisted quietly.

"Oh, yes, Theodosia made that *quite* clear, but Letty said it ought to stay in the family, even after my death, even though that Charlotte family hasn't even got the same name."

"And was Mrs. Dunham here the same afternoon the will was signed?"

"It was signed after dinner, here in the parlor."

"On the evening of the same day that Mrs. Dunham was here?"

"Yes — yes, it must have been."

"I see. All this is very useful, you know, you're being

[225]

a big help. Now, what did Miss Theodosia do with the will when she had finished discussing it with you and Mrs. Dunham?"

"What did she . . . ?" Miss Miranda had lost the thread.

"Did she put it away in her desk? Or did she leave it with you to put somewhere? Or — "

"Oh, she gave it back to them."

Ridge sat very still.

"She gave it back to the Watsons between the time that she talked to Mrs. Dunham about it and the time she signed it?"

"Yes. He wanted to make a copy of it. Mr. Granger, I mean."

"About what time of day would that be?"

"Well, I don't know when he copied it, I suppose — "

"No, I meant — about when did she give it back to them?"

"After Letty Dunham had gone. She didn't stay long, either, because it was such a tiff. She wouldn't even stop for a cup of tea."

"Then it was tea-time when she left."

"Yes — very nearly."

"Then the Watsons must have had the will in their possession for several hours — between tea-time and that evening after dinner."

"Yes — of course. Or Mr. Granger had it, I suppose."

"And later that same evening it was brought out for her to sign."

"Yes — on account of the Smiths leaving the next day. They witnessed it."

"Miss Miranda — did either you or your sister read the will before she signed it?"

"Why, I've just been telling you — we were reading it that afternoon when Letty Dunham came in — "

"But just before she signed it that evening, here in the parlor — did she read it then?"

"No, because we'd been all over it, only a little while before."

"That's fine," said Ridge, and rose in a leisurely way. "We're doing fine. I haven't seen Mrs. Dunham around lately, has she been ill?"

"Oh, no, Letty's never ill — she went to Charleston for a visit. She told me at the funeral she was going to see her daughter's new baby, the next day."

"*Another* baby?" said Ridge with marked surprise.

"That's three! I expect to hear all about it in a day or two. Letty must be home again now."

Extricating himself without visible haste, Ridge got into his little second-hand car and headed it for Live Oaks, where the Dunhams lived.

XXIV

Letty Dunham was one of those dear women. Everything about her was kind and good-tempered and sensible. Although her bags were not yet unpacked from the Charleston visit, she received Ridge cordially and invited him to stay to lunch, which was now falling due.

Faced with the alternative of making her go hungry after her journey while he asked tedious questions beyond the range of the servant's ears, or containing himself until after the meal, he chose lunch, and passed an agreeable and illuminating hour hearing all about babies, and about Letty Dunham's remarkable grandchildren in particular. When they rose from the table he stood before her with his best smile and asked if he might speak to her in the parlor.

"I thought you had something on your mind," she remarked, and led the way.

He explained briefly about the will proceedings, and Mrs. Dunham was astonished to hear that there was any question of Miss Miranda's rights.

"Is *that* what it is!" she exclaimed. "My husband wrote me that the will was being contested, but I thought of course that was the cousin who had been disinherited, the one up in Charlotte — you might expect him to make a fuss."

"He hasn't been heard from," said Ridge. "Miss Miranda says you happened in during the afternoon when they were discussing the will."

"Yes, I did. I'm afraid I rather spoke my mind," Mrs. Dunham smiled sadly. "It was none of my business, of course, what Theodosia chose to do in her will. But it did take me by surprise that she would even consider those dreadful people as her heirs."

"Had you met the Watsons?" Ridge had not expected this.

"Oh, yes, the year before, and it was really disgusting the way they played up to those two little ninnies — making such a fuss over everything from the furniture to the cooking. The Sibley girls have always been house-proud, and it was just the sort of thing they would fall for."

"Then you think the Watsons had this thing in mind as long ago as last year."

"Well, I didn't suspect what they were up to, of course, till that day I caught Theodosia with the will. But I never liked what little I saw of them, they seemed to me a good deal worse than most of the hunting crowd who come down here."

"That's very interesting," said Ridge thoughtfully.

"What on earth do they want with a place like Chimneys?" Mrs. Dunham demanded sensibly. "Not to live in, surely!"

"I think there was a project to turn it into some sort of club," Ridge said tentatively.

"Oh, heavens, we can't have anything like that in the neighborhood, can we! Besides, where would they get the money?"

"What money?" asked Ridge, fascinated, leading her on.

"The money to finance and run any such enterprise," said Mrs. Dunham impatiently. "It would take a lot of capital to get a thing like that going."

"And you don't think the Watsons have capital?"

"Why, of course not, you can tell by looking at them that they aren't the real millionaire type."

Ridge gazed at her with admiration.

"How?" he asked. "How can you tell?"

"By the way they dress and the way they speak, and the way they have with servants!" Mrs. Dunham threw out her hands in a gesture of exasperation and amusement. "*They're* not Park Avenue or Long Island. They're *little* people. They're after something. I tried to tell Theodosia so, but she wouldn't listen."

"It appears," said Ridge thoughtfully, "that you saw at a glance what it is going to take several days in court to prove."

"What do you mean — that they're fakes?"

"Something like that. Now, as I understand it, Miss Theodosia was going over the will with her sister when you arrived?"

"Yes, she had the papers in her hand. I gathered it was

only a draft that she hadn't signed, which was why I put in my two cents' worth."

"And did you gather that Miss Miranda was provided for during her lifetime in the will as it stood then?"

"Oh, yes, that was understood. I didn't read it myself, because it wasn't offered, but Theodosia got very vexed with me when I objected to the Watson people coming after Miranda instead of the Charlotte cousins. There was never any question of the Watsons coming *before* her, in Theodosia's mind."

"Mm-hm," said Ridge, with satisfaction. "That's what we want to know. Thank you very much." He rose.

"Can I do anything more?" Mrs. Dunham offered anxiously.

"You can come into court and say what you have just said to me about the provision for Miss Miranda, please."

"I'll be glad to."

"I think," said Ridge, "we've got something now."

Mr. Conway thought so too. Stimulated by their prospects, he was in fine form during the opening routine of the trial, and conducted a brisk cross-examination of the Smiths, who appeared as the first witnesses for the Watsons.

It was not until they put Mrs. Dunham on the stand and began to lead her through the account of her visit to Miss Theodosia that he seemed to falter, and only a minute later he dropped back into his chair and motioned Ridge up to his place. Ridge took over smoothly, putting the questions as planned and receiving her direct and damaging replies, and they had nearly finished when the attack gripped Mr. Conway. Ridge was instantly at his side, snapping the tiny glass phial in the handkerchief and moving the fragrant stuff back and forth in front of Mr. Conway's face, while the older man sat motionless, pale and drawn, breathing cautiously, enduring the pain.

Court was recessed for the day, and a call was put in for the doctor, already out on an emergency. Letty Dunham helped Ridge to get Mr. Conway home in his car and to bed. There was no doubt about the doctor's verdict when he came. So far as Mr. Conway was concerned, the Sibley will case was closed.

"He wants you to go ahead tomorrow as though you had conducted it all along," the doctor reported to Ridge in the Conway parlor later that evening.

"But that's impossible, sir, tomorrow is the day he was going to spring Wilson on them."

"Spring him on them yourself," said the doctor. "You found him, didn't you?"

"Yes, but — this is much too important a thing for me to handle alone, I might make a mess of it."

"None of that, now," the doctor said severely. "*He* says you can do it. Show him."

"But poor Miss Miranda — she counts on him — "

"She'll trust you in his place, if he says so."

"Oh, Lord, I shall be numb with fright," said Ridge. "May I go up and see him?"

"Not tonight. I've just got him quiet, by promising him

that you'd go ahead tomorrow. He said above all not to let Wilkins know if you're worried."

"*Worried!*" said Ridge. "What kind of a word is that!"

"Go home and rehearse Wilkins," said the doctor. "I'll be there in court tomorrow morning, and I want to see you come out swinging."

XXV

A<small>ND THE WAY THEY LOOKED,</small>" <small>YOUNG MR.</small>
Wilkins was saying for the fourth or fifth time, "when you
suddenly produced *me*, like a rabbit out of a hat, I shall
never forget as long as I live! You know, I wasn't a bit
nervous once I got started, though I expected to be scared
out of my mind — I expect that's the way you handled it,
really, you were so calm about it, you didn't give me any
chance to get the jitters. . . ."

They were sitting in Alice's room near midnight of the
following day, at the table which held the lamp and a decanter, and their half-empty glasses, and Mr. Wilkins
though not by any means drunk was still glowing and talkative from the unaccustomed limelight. When they left the
courtroom they had gone first with the doctor straight to
Mr. Conway's house, and found him sitting propped up in
bed expecting them. He insisted that everybody should
have a drink at his bedside — not to celebrate the verdict,
which he maintained came as no surprise to him, but in
honor of the junior partnership he was offering Ridge.

Then the doctor had put a firm end to the excitement

[234]

there and carried Ridge off to dinner at his home, still towing Mr. Wilkins, because Ridge had driven him into town that morning and his car was therefore still at Avalon, where he would spend at least this one more night. The moon was rising in the spring night sky when they at last drove homeward, a little limp with reaction, but quite sober, and full of a solemn, sublime satisfaction.

On the table in the hall at Avalon, standing up against the lamp where Jeb had propped it to catch Ridge's eye, was a letter from Mary. He saw as he slipped it into his coat pocket that it was postmarked Washington, but young Mr. Wilkins was still on his hands, wide awake and talkative, and looking as though he expected yet another drink. With Mary's letter unopened in his pocket, Ridge had got out the decanter and the glasses and resigned himself to wait until his guest showed signs of running down, or going off to bed.

Almost he was glad of a period of respite before he must read the letter. Almost he wished there was someone, impersonal and kind, to whom he could hand the sealed envelope and say, "Read it to me — just say Yes or No — " He was inordinately tired, and keyed up, and he had had all that was bearable for one day. To learn now that he had lost Mary would, he felt, snap something inside him that was stretched much too tight, and while the resulting let-down would be in its way a relief, he yielded almost willingly to a cowardly postponement. To the possibility that he had not lost her after all, he closed his mind, on the theory that you didn't hit bottom so hard if you always expected the worst.

It was just the bitter way things work out, he was prepared to find, that by the time he had finally accumulated the bare minimum it was possible to offer her, someone else should come along and treble his bid. Had he, this time, won the battle and lost the war?

"And when I *think*," young Mr. Wilkins's voice ran on beside him, "that if I hadn't just happened to come over here from the Beach on spec, as a matter of fact, hoping to pick up enough dollars to stay in the South a bit longer because I do love it so down here, and it *would* have been a nice job at the Sibley place if they could have gone through with it without dislocating poor Miss Miranda — when I *think* that but for that little coincidence those dreadful people would have actually brought it off and she would be right out in the cold for the rest of her life — because it was my testimony that turned the trick, wasn't it! — it does make you think, doesn't it, almost as though there really was some kind of *design* — as though we don't really decide these things for ourselves, however much we may think we do — and then your happening to speak to me like that at the hotel, and just by *accident* saying something that made me mention the Sibley house, or you might never have known — oh, no, you did know, didn't you! — did you speak to me *on purpose*, then, I'm getting all mixed up. . . ."

Ridge filled Mr. Wilkins's glass. No hurry. There was a

design. The letter in his pocket was part of it. Opening the letter now, or an hour from now, wouldn't change that. She had come to him, she had lighted his way, and because of her the dreadful descent to Avernus had been checked and he was safe now, safe from the old horror and despair, no matter what happened. Yes, even without her, now he had fashioned some sort of life, something to go on with, something to hold to — perhaps that was the design — perhaps only that. Perhaps to gain back his soul from the pit and reach for heaven too was unreasonable. . . .

"Oh, I keep meaning to ask you," Mr. Wilkins recollected suddenly — "What becomes of the Watsons now? I mean, what we did this afternoon isn't the end, is it? Won't they have to go to jail, I hope?"

"It's a case for the district attorney now," said Ridge, with a small grim smile. "We can't arrest them, if that's what you mean. But as we consider there is definite evidence of criminality, we turn over the record to the district attorney and stand ready to co-operate."

"But they *will* be brought to trial for trying to swindle Miss Miranda, won't they?"

"I hope so. But it's out of our hands now. We saved the house for her, that's the main thing."

"You know what I bet could be proved?" said Mr. Wilkins. "I bet the district attorney, or whoever, could prove that the whole trip down here was just a plant, a frame-up, to get hold of the house. I bet that Mr. What's-his-name that went to California so he couldn't be produced at the trial was no lawyer at all, he was just one of the gang made up like a lawyer. I bet he never typed out any wills at all when he borrowed Mr. Smith's typewriter — I bet he had written both wills already, before they ever came here, and all he did was sit up there in his room and write Now-is-the-time-for-all-good-men-to-come-to-the-aid-of-the-party to make it *seem* as though he was writing a will — and I bet if Miss Theodosia had just *happened* to stop and read the will she signed before she signed it, *none* of this would have happened!" He paused dramatically, waiting for comment.

"I expect you're right," said Ridge, rousing himself. "They were taking quite a risk, but it was all in the way they handled it, of course — she wouldn't have stood a chance, they could have stage-managed her right out of her eye-teeth, and very nearly did."

"You know, I got the most tremendous kick out of watching you this afternoon," Mr. Wilkins rambled on. "You suddenly came over all Jehovian and terrible, like the wrath of God, without ever raising your voice. You'd make a wonderful hanging judge. I suddenly realized this afternoon that lawyers are rather like actors, really, they have to know their timing, and the way to make a point, and how to get a laugh in the right place. . . . But you must be dead tired, you had the whole thing on your shoulders, and here I sit gabbling — I suppose we must go to bed and try to sleep it off, I mean I'm not a bit drunk, I think I have a sort of nerve-jag, now that it's all over and we've won. I hope poor little Miss Miranda is all tucked up tight asleep in her little bed, with her beautiful house all safe around her — and all thanks to you. You know, bringing off a thing like that today must make you feel rather like a general when he lays out a campaign — I mean, when it really comes off, you know, like Washington up at Yorktown, winning the battle just the way he had planned it. Only the way you led them on today was rather more like an ambush, wasn't it, you got them all wound up in their own statements and then *boom*. I almost wish I'd gone in for law myself, I never realized till today what a wonderful profession it can be — what a power for good against evil. You must be very proud, at a time like this, and yet there you sit, no different from me, not a bit excited or above yourself. I suppose lawyers get used to pulling people out of holes and having them cry all over you with gratitude — "

Proud. Yes, but not excited any more. Perhaps never any more, if Mary was gone. But proud, yes, because she had believed in him and been willing to trust her life to him when he had less than nothing to offer. Proud for Mary, and for Mr. Conway, who had gambled on him when he wasn't worth a nickel. And for the Colonel. Did he know? He would have liked that bit about Yorktown. . . .

There was someone else who would appreciate Mr. Wilkins's artless joke, somewhere in the shades. Once more, the lamplight and his own fatigue were playing tricks with Ridge's fancy, so that he knew very well who had planned the campaign and whose generalship had won the battle in that courtroom — and he was more than ready to assign his own laurels to a bold and lighthearted strategist dead a hundred and seventy years. He would never suspect, even by daylight, that generalship was also in the blood and bone of Ridge Creston, waiting to be called on.

"Well, this ought to be a lesson to me, the company I keep," young Wilkins was saying, glass in hand. "Still, it brought me here, and that is one of the nicest things that ever happened to me. But if I outstay my welcome I'll never get asked back again, will I, so I'm going straight off to bed this minute, you must be dropping with exhaustion, so if you'll excuse me now I'll say good-night. . . ."

He rose, not quite steadily, and Ridge rose too, serene and smiling, and saw him to the staircase with his candle. Then he returned to the lamp on the table in Alice's room, and sat down and opened Mary's letter.

It wasn't very long.

DEAR RIDGE — MY DARLING RIDGE — I have been and seen and done, as you asked me to. It has all been very charming, and expensive, and luxurious, and Alec has been the soul of kindness and discretion. I am very glad that I did it, like leaving no stone unturned, and I am flying back tomorrow morning to spend the rest of my vacation at home, as I promised them I would.

And now perhaps you will believe me when I say that it's you I want, and whatever goes with you, and no matter how long we have to wait for it. I think it was the General who saw to that. You said once I was in love with him, and I guess in a way I was, then. Maybe you thought when I saw a real general, I'd have to be in love with him too. And I guess in some ways Alec is a lot like him. But if that is so, then my General knew very well what he was doing about that too. Look, my girl, he said, this is how soldiers are — you wouldn't care for it, not to live with, it's not what you want, in your right mind —— I showed you what you want, in South Carolina, and it's still there — take it with my love, he said, you're grown up now.

That's how it is, Ridge. Are you terribly disappointed not to be rid of me, after all?

MARY

And because he was really very tired, and the tight-stretched something inside him had let go very gently, instead of rending asunder in a loud annihilating sheet of pain, he put his head on his arms on the table above Mary's letter with a thankfulness too wide and deep for any coherent thought or expression. Jeb found him like that, motionless, but far from asleep, when he looked in at the door to see if it was time to put out the lamp.